# Trans-4-ma-tion
# 2

By: Austin P.

This novel is a work of fiction, any resemblance to real people, living or dead, actual events, establishments, organizations, or locales are intended to give the fiction a sense of reality and authenticity. Other names of characters, places, and incidents are either products of the author's imagination or are used fictitiously. Those fictionalized events and incidents that include real persons DID NOT OCCUR and may not be used as if it did.



ISBN- 978-1542505178
ISBN-10: 1542505178

**Contact Information:**
KBA Publications
P.O. Box 2863
Phenix City, AL 36868

Printed in the USA

# TRANS-4-MA-TION

# ACKNOWLEDGMENTS

I want to thank God for still having me amongst the land of the living. I would also like to thank God for being my protector, provider, and for his precious guidance. Listen, Super Counselor put me in the Hole. It was not where I wanted to be, but where I needed to be. I won back my health by exercising and fasting. The microwaved food and radiation processed meat took a major toll on my body; causing me to have severe acid reflex and having to burp a lot. I began to focus more on the Lord. Once again, I was blessed with the beautiful opportunity to always search for something positive out of a negative situation.

I told myself, "Let's birth Trans-4-Mation 2, so I can continue to share with the world that my God is Almighty and Awesome."

Now, as a male evolved into a man, he will always think about the consequences and know that his mother, wife, and children are with him for better or worse. Meaning, if or once he does something crazy, he will be dragging his love ones down the drain with him. A man will forget about all the bad habits and characteristics he learned or inherited. He will be himself. He will go about the walk of life to better his condition. Overall, he will see the bigger picture and know he cannot do anything without the Godly eyes. He will not disrespect anyone, because he knows he will be disrespecting himself. It is easy to be a male, but a tough thing to be a man because you will have to put all childish things to the side. Have you heard the saying, you can't send a boy to do a man's job? A man will become productive instead of destructive. He will lead by good examples. He will be a good provider and guide for his family; he wouldn't want his offspring or following generation to repeat his tragedy to become their occupation. Any male can be a daddy, but it will take a man to become a father in addition to raise a child. As a troubled youngster, I was lost, confused, and stayed doing all the wrong things. It took me over forty years to find my purpose in life. That is to say; It's never too late. When I look back on my BS life, from the negative individual I used to be, compared to the positive person I am today, I thank God for not letting me down nor turning his back on me. I thank God for continuing to work with me and for turning my dreams and vision into reality. Now, I just work each day to change tomorrow. I have been in prison for over two decades, straight!!! By the grace of God, I never gave up on my life. God picked me up, carried me, coached me, and most of all protected me.

No matter what you do in life, you will always have the haters to sharpen you. Guys say that I can't write. My brothers from different mothers say I need to stop writing, but it does not offend me, because this is God's work. God also asks, how is it possible for one to love Him and not love your neighbor? So, with that being said, to the haters, I sincerely hope and pray this novel or one of my other novels awaken the youth, our upcoming generation. In addition to someone in your family, because there is nothing cool about coming to jail or prison, trying to be the bad guy, or dying young. And now, with all due respect, I don't want to further delay any of you away from the fruit of my beautiful labor.........

## To the Blind

You wanna be a killer? A drug dealer?
Take it from the horse's mouth; it'll be wise to reconsider.
The White House knows there will never be another Obama
We are killing our race off winter, spring, fall, and especially in the summer.
When one female is killed, it'll destroy a whole nation
The blind can no longer lead the younger generation
Why we only wake up after a tragedy or our trial and tribulations
Please, people, let's stay on reality, I have been held hostage
Absent for over 2-decades, away from my family and society
From my bad boy walks in life, now all I got is stories to tell
Class is in session, so ring the school bell.

Wisdom - the ability to understand what is right, true, enduring. Good judgement. (Webster's)

Wisdom – knowledge in action of living that involves intelligence, integrity, morals, and principles. (Hebrew Translation)

Wisdom is knowledge/education gained, put into action practiced/experienced, once understood, then passed on.

It is not the knowledge itself, but what is done with the knowledge, that separates the wise from the fool. A wise man knows that a treasure shared has more value. A fool only believes that true jewels should be buried and kept in secret, hidden, and should die along with the fool, himself. To pass on wisdom (knowledge) is one of the ways of serving the Creator because it is only from Him, who created us, that we received this. It is our servitude to raise our aptitude and show gratitude, by freely sharing and passing on his knowledge and power. Power should never be subdued (brought under control by force). It takes away from its nature and purpose.

God speaks through my sinful body; my flesh and spirit are weak. Jesus fed bread and fish; I need everyone to continue to eat.

Lord, I pray to you from every Tuesday to Tuesday, asking for your forgiveness and for you to use me.
Now, I face reality, if there was no you, God, there wouldn't be any me.

Thank you, my merciful Lord, for the absence of society…Now, I am much better than I used to be. I know you're still working with me.

My trials and tribulations are education. The creator said share the word, so I made writing and speaking my occupation, no longer yielding to temptation.

I pray day-to-day, begging for my sins to be washed away. I changed for the best; I don't care what one must have to say.
I used to think I was hard, I knew I wasn't smart. I was too cowardly to try talking to you, my Lord.

To my partners in crime, let's capitalize from our

mistakes. Please, allow me to introduce you to ALLAH.

Cause if it ain't about God, I'm straight. Remember, It's never too late. Come to God when you get tired of the devil baking you a cake.

If I hadn't gotten locked up, I would have missed my blessing. The same one protecting Moses from Pharaoh secures me with protection…

# CHAPTER 1

Chase sat on the lower bunk of the bunk bed that was mounted to the wall. There were matching steel, open face drawers also mounted to the bottom of the beds, for each person to have his own individual drawer to place his personal belongings.

The left-hand side of the six-by-six cell was a steel desk mounted to the wall, the steel seat was mounted to the desk, but could be pushed in or out from underneath the desk as needed. The six-foot-long light was mounted above the desk and was protected by steel and plexiglass to keep the insane from tampering with or destroying the lights.

Approximately two feet over sat the steel sink and commode, which was mounted to the wall as well. Above the sink was another three-foot mounted light, protected by the steel and plexiglass as well. No more than two and a half feet away was the six-foot steel door painted blue, same as the bunk beds. Five feet up the door, there was about a three-hand-and-a-half size plexiglass, so the staff could peek in on you, when they made their rounds. Next to the window was a square-shaped place to speak through the door. Above the door were thirty-three holes of an air conditioner. When the air became too cold, the guys would use tissue to cut off as much air as needed. The right side of the room was nothing but a steel wall that will drive one crazy if he doesn't have a very strong mind to cope.

Chase rubbed his head because, in the blink of an eye, his life has slipped through his fingertips. One bad decision, one bad choice had cost him his freedom. Now, all kinds of positive things stormed through his mind, and that made things even harder. He asked the white officer to give him a couple of cups of water, and once the mission was accomplished, Chase thanked him, and the C.O. replied,

"You're most welcome."

Chase later asked three black COs and got turned down by all three. Here, majority of the black staff gave a black guy HELL. They would go all out of their way to make your life miserable, as if some of them were racist towards their own people. There were also the Caucasian staff that would give the black guys the blues… they will be laying in the cut, hoping and praying for the opportunity to arrive, so they can skin you alive. As they say, there are nine ways to skin a cat, and for something petty, one's going to experience all nine of the ways. In prison, one would get write-ups for various reasons: he'll lose six months' commissary, six months' visitation, six months' phone, six months' use of e-mails, and twenty-seven days of hole time. Majority of the time, no matter the reason, one is going to lose all privileges as well as good time. Guys can get caught horse playing, and get their privileges taken as well as lose good time. When these days of good time are taken, that means that those same days will be added to one's own sentence and must do those days again.

Chase's thoughts were interrupted as the same voice, as always, reported, "We got one!"

The guy was letting everyone know someone was coming to the SHU. He had a window view of the whole compound. The compound was so small that one could stand anywhere and watch the entire compound.

"Put him in here with me so that I can make love to him," shouted the same insane guy. He'd make that ugly statement about guys that he didn't know, and who didn't know him or couldn't recognize his voice. Little did the young brother know, that type of language was only acceptable here, because anywhere else, one of the guy's homies would have put him on blast and made his homie body bag him. If not, he would've tried to.

Under no circumstances was crazy language acceptable without a killing, stabbing, or all-out car war. The guys could and would care less about who's one of Jerry Lewis or Bonnie Fife's babies. Being under the psychologist's care still didn't stop anything. These people saw blood, smelled blood, tasted blood, and craved only to waste blood.

All problems were solved by warring and bloodshed. For big problems as well as small problems, violence is the correct formula.

The COs began to take the guys out to rec, which consisted of six cages that could hold around ten guys, but they only put six in so they could walk, exercise, or stand by the cage next to them and talk without having to get out of the next man's way. The COs often try to deceive the prisoners by saying it was colder than what it was, so hopefully, fewer people would go out. It would mean less work on their behalf.

"L.E.S., what up, bru?"

"What up, son?" L.E.S. greeted back.

"Te-To, what's up, big guy?"

"Alright, going out to get some of this fresh air," Te-To replied.

"Dread. What's up, bru?"

"What's up, what's up," Dread responded, and continued talking his famous sports language with the guys. He was determined to state facts about why his team was going to win before he even reaches the coat rack.

"Valentine, what's up?" someone hollered.

Valentino looked around for his friend, because he was no stranger to that voice and besides, this was the only guy who pronounced his name that way.

"Where are you, old man?" Valentino's voice echoed.

"I'm up here!" the guy shouted, as he repeatedly banged on the plexiglass, trying to indicate he was on the top range.

He only had Valentino by seven or eight years, but Valentino always greeted him by Old Man.

"You coming outside?" Valentino asked.

"Too cold. I don't come out on the compound when it's cold. Jack Frost the man, and I respect his gangsta."

When guys come back in, they'll be exchanging complaints. My nose is cold. My ears are cold. My toes are cold. My feet are cold.

Each person has a towel over their head. They're not equipped with enough gear to temper with Mr. Jack Frost in the first place; they just don't want to allow the COs to violate one of their rights that they have coming.

"Bruce, Bruce, what it do?"

"What up doe?" Bruce replied.

"D-Town! You escaped me from that one-on-one."

"I'm a Gangsta, you can't win against me," Bruce said, with confidence.

The guy saw Young Fresh from the Ham going to rec, so he threw the challenge in that direction.

"Fresh. I'll take you in basketball."

"I already did beat you twice! I skunked you one game. Man, you can't fuck with a baby picture of me," Fresh said. Skunk means that the opponent did not score one point throughout the entire game.

"Young Buck, I'm old enough to be your daddy. You don't get no points for beating me; you already know that."

"Your old ass needs to stay in your old ass lane," Fresh stated, and added, "I refuse to let an old man beat me in anything."

"Frank, what's up?" He greeted the oldest guy that was a part of the Florida car. He used to play basketball on Frank's basketball team. That's how he tore the tendon in his knee.

"How's the leg coming?" Frank asked out of concern and predicted, "You'll be playing again by the summer."

"Frank, I'm done like Jordan. I hung my tennis shoes up.

My basketball playing days are long over with now."

"Not mines," Frank announced and threw a comment for anyone to accept the challenge. "I ain't gonna let a youngster beat me at nothing."

Stank was heading down the runway. "Tank, what's up? What up with that boy Jack Rabbit," the guy greeted, and asked about Tank's partner.

"He sent me a check," Stank publicized, not caring if addressed by Stank or Tank.

"That's what he's supposed to do."

"Sin City. You have been mighty quiet up there. What you doing?"

"Pushing my pen, so I can get me a check."

Two cousins walked by, so the guy directed his attention to them.

"Marcus and Pete. What's up, homies?"

"What up," they both greeted, in unison.

He also greeted E, from Florida. "E, what's up, homie?"

"What's up, homie?" E. said, returning the same greeting.

"How many more do we have to take out?" the CO, with the limp in his walk, asked. "This is it," The CO confirmed, as he was coming down the stairs with shitty ass Twin, aka the blind lead the blind, birds of a feather flock together.

Due to this white CO always being polite and very, very respectful, as well as being determined to give the prisoners everything they have coming, they nicknamed him 'The People's Champ.' If someone did want to do something crazy or talk crazy, they wouldn't do it to this officer, because nobody would allow them to. This CO's demeanor all around the board was a positive force field.

"Gentlemen, they saved the shittiest for last." He saluted Twin. "Boy, you were playing Russian Rolette with six bullets in the chamber, due to your absence of knowledge, you became famous. Shitty ass Twin, if you were running for president, you wouldn't have gotten my vote."

This place was a holding facility, a transit center. They housed prisoners here until they were transported, but they were here for various reasons. Some were here awaiting trial; others until they were transported to their designation. On the other hand, some guys were waiting to go to the free world doctors. Big Rock, from Augusta, Georgia, arrived early that morning. Chase overheard him telling their neighbor that he'd be going to the outside hospital in the morning and that he'd only be there for one night. Chase noticed when Rock came in that he grabbed a Bible, and later that night, he asked for a cowboy novel to read.

"One book the way of life, and the other one to help kill the clock," Chase said, thinking out loud.

He also was waiting to kill the clock, because his first love had told him they would pray every night at 9 p.m. She informed Chase that prayer changes things and that God is a good God. A merciful God. That everyone should take their problems and burdens to God because God has the power to do the most mysterious things. God can touch other people's hearts and give them a change of heart. And that God is the best of planners. God sees into the future, and what God has planned, no one nor nothing can stop it. Once the clock struck 9 p.m., Chase dropped to both knees, getting into his prayer position. He wanted to pray many times before, but he was ashamed because he didn't know how to pray or what to say. Now, Chase was prepared to do what the wise men do, which was to seek counseling, protection, and guidance. Chase knew he needed the same one who protected Moses from Pharaoh. Here and now, he allowed the words to escape his two lips freely.

"My precious and Almighty Lord. I kneel before you tonight asking for your forgiveness. For your assistance. For your aid. For your guidance. I was always told to come to you with all my problems, big or small. God, I'm a sinner who has nowhere else to go. My Lord, strengthen me, guide me, and please use my sinful body as a vessel, so I can become a blessing to others as you have become a blessing for me. God, please hear and accept my prayer. I want to become one of your servants. I was once told that if I become one of your worshipers, that you will answer my prayers…"

The more Chase prayed the lighter his heart became, and he looked forward to praying. Lionel Ritchie's beautiful song constantly stayed in his heart, mouth, and mind.

"Call on him in the morning?"
"JESUS!"
"Call on him in the midnight hours?"
"JESUS!"
"Who can bring you joy?"
"JESUS!"
"Who can turn your life around?"
"JESUS!"

The female food server informer, Ms. Keiara, took pride in her cooking. She had a passion for cooking, and as the country slogan goes, she put her feet into the meals. She did not just throw the meals together as the other food service informer had. She cooked for the inmates as though she was cooking for herself or her family.

Ms. Keiara, she took an extra mile when she didn't have to. The food was seasoned good, and where it would only cost two dollars to feed each inmate, she upped the ante by two dollars, giving the inmates a healthy four-dollar meal. In other prisons, they did not feed this good. Hamburger day consisted of two patties and not one. She gave onion rings and French fries. Fish day consisted of three pieces the size of a forearm. Fried chicken was two giant pieces. Breakfast day was four link sausages, four scrambled eggs, hash browns, and a bowl of cheese grits. When pancakes or waffles were served, there were always four of them, the size of the plate. Two of the giant babies would have done the job alone. When the other food service informers don't feed as she does, the prisoners are always whining and complaining instead of counting their blessings, as well as looking at the situation as being a privilege to have had the meals during her work days. Sometimes, people can be ungrateful, especially when they're a little bird in a nest.

"I'm gonna ask the brother on this shift to give me some water and I'ma see what he'll have to say. I've got nothing to lose and everything to gain. Besides, a closed mouth can't get fed. Peter and Paul said try'em all." Chase said to himself.

CO Gee was walking down Chase's range.

"Yo, CO?"

"Yeah, what's up?"

"Man, I need you to give me two cups of water."

"Ya water doesn't work in there?"

"Man, this water has too much lead in it, every time I drink this water, it hurts my stomach and leaves a bad taste in my mouth."

"The same water you have in there is the same water out here."

"Man, the white CO gave me some, and that water out there is better."

"It's all coming out the same pipes!"

"All I need is two cups," Chase pleaded, as the CO popped the slot and collected Chase's two cups, and moments later, returned with the cups full of water.

"Man, this is the most stupid shit I have ever done."

"Naw, CO, it's one of the best things that you have ever done," Chase replied. "God's going to bless you for your good deed. That's how we gain blessings, by assisting the people."

Chase had gotten smart and made a flush sign, so any time he needed his toilet flushed, he 'd just have to push the sign through the door. This would eliminate him from having to holler that he needed a flush, or having to stand by the door and wait on the COs to make around, so he could get his toilet flushed.

"God put bruh here so that he could be a blessing to me, and God put me here, so bruh could make a blessing off me. So, we were a blessing for one another," Chase said, smiling as well as counting his blessing.

YOU CAN BE
THE ARCHITECT
TO YOUR LIFE...

YOUR DECISIONS
AND CHOICES
ARE VERY PRECIOUS.

# CHAPTER 2

Mr. Pete and Baltimore Rick sat on the steel table, Shakur sat on the steel bench. Sten parked his wheelchair next to Mr. Pete. They were enjoying the fresh air, and one another's company, as always. Shakur spotted the school teacher, as she was making her way through the gate.

"Here comes Ms. AB, coming to find her students."

"That's a good thing. They need to be in class to get their education," stated Mr. Pete.

"That's the key to success," Sten X added.

"Without an education, there isn't much one can do," said Baltimore Rick.

Everyone spoke and joked with Ms. AB, but little did she know, she was well respected and highly appreciated. They always gave her a round of applause, as she escorted her students off to the rec yard and back to the schoolhouse.

G-Jeez always forced her to come find him. He was good for skipping the G.E.D. class twice a week.... and Ms. AB had no problems with finding him twice a week.

"Ms. AB, you looking for your students?" Carlos yelled.

"Yes," she answered.

"Which one? The one that doesn't know his ABC's?" Carlos' question session began.

"No, Marcus is in the classroom already."

“Oh,” Carlos smacked his forehead, “You are looking for the one who doesn't know his times tables?” he said, forcing Ms. AB to sly way snitch.

“That's Jap, he's in the classroom also,” Ms. AB said, smiling.

Her students tell her everything. They talked to her as if she was one of the inmates. She knows everything that goes on, on the compound. She knows every one of her students’ business. One of her students told her his girlfriend left him, Ms. AB predicted because he'd been in the G.E.D. class for five years and his old lady wanted a man who was trying to learn something, so he can come home better than he left. Women want men with some skills and trades under their belt.

“I'm looking for them K-2 babies,” Ms. AB addressed the two students, as they nicknamed themselves. “They already don't use their brain; now they're trying to put a hole in it. They get that toolie, mix it with the woolie, and act the foolie...”

“Not the two!” someone hollered.

G-Jeez was waiting on his turn to hit the two when Ms. AB spotted him.

“Come on, K-2 baby!” she publicized, waving him towards her.

There was one way in and one way out, so she posted herself by the gate. G-Jeez knew better than to prolong her, because it would attract the rec officer.

“I'm coming,” he said, acknowledging her, so she'd keep

her distance and hopefully stop putting him on blast.

"Come on. You don't need another hit of that K-2, because one hit is too many, and it'll have ya mouth stankin' and ya finger tips brown," Ms. AB said, letting G-Jeez know that she was hip to him.

"Calm down; I'm coming," G-Jeez shouted.

"Man, you gotta get the fuck on. You are going to fuck around and blow up the spot. We don't need the spot hot," one of the off-brand smokers said.

"Damn man! I'm tired of that woman always looking for me," G-Jeez replied, with an attitude.

Ms. AB's presence blew his high. It was already hard to catch a good high with four guys trying to get a pull on a five-dollar stick, which consisted of a couple of sprinkles of spice that was half the size of a watch battery.

"What is a three-letter word that means the same as a couple?" Ms. AB shouted over to G-Jeez to see if he still knew the answer. He did not guess the right answer. After twelve wrong answers, Ms. AB told him it was "a few."

"Few," G-Jeez immediately replied.

"Good," Ms. AB said, clapping, "Now, your few minutes are up, let's go to the classroom, cause the fellows are waiting on me and you."

"They in there playing Slap Hands or Spades, if they ain't talking about what's happenin' on the compound," G-Jeez said.

"True that," Ms. AB said, using their language. "But what goes on in the classroom, stays in the classroom."

G-Jeez's big homie walked over and kicked him so hard in the butt, that dust jumped off the seat of his pants. As soon as G-Jeez turned to face him, he slapped G-Jeez across the head.

"Boy, you always out here talking shit about your teacher. She comes out here to get your uneducated ass because she wants to see you do better. She wants better for you than what you want for your damn self! Boy, that white woman comes out here to get ya blue, black ass when she doesn't have to, because her classroom is going to go on with or without you. And she's still going to get paid. You're very unappreciative. That teacher has begun to look at her students as her children, as her family! She got love for y'all, and y'all show her love in return by disrespecting her. Allow her to teach you some sense."

G-Jeez walked over to Ms. AB with his head down and mumbled, "I'm sorry for having you walk down here to get me."

"I look forward to the walk," Ms. AB said, smiling. "K-2 baby, you have to start thinking outside the box. And if you're looking for a leader to follow in here, then please follow the leader that you see when you look into the mirror."

From that day forward, Ms. AB's students, as well as the compound, began calling her 'Momma AB.' They began to put forth the effort to learn, and her student's numbers began to change dramatically. She had more students to pass the G.E.D because they wanted to do it for her more than they wanted to do it for themselves.

"Ms. AB is a good woman, may God bless her heart," Larry Williams, aka Neo, said.

"God made her a blessing, so she'll become a blessing to others," Mr. Carter said.

"We need more teachers like her in this compound," Shakur said, "By her showing the young brothers that she cares about them, causes them to change their ungodly ways out of feeling guilty for themselves."

"I'm going to go around the track a few times," Sten X said, "I can use a little bit of exercise."

"A little bit beats nothing at all, Brother Sten," Mr. Pete encouraged.

Shakur overlooked C and B Rec yard. Mr. Ben was on C yard schooling the young buck. They always stayed in Mr. Ben's presence, and that told him that they were trying to change.

"Youngsters, if y'all can get y'all's points down, get away from here. It's a danger spot because when it goes down, it's going down. A lot of good guys are going to get caught up. A lot of them going to die." While Mr. Ben was giving the lecture, he watched the young Mexican, and a no-brainer brother argue back and forth.

He hoped and prayed what looked like it was about to happen would not happen. This was about to unfold behind a room sale. True enough, Wrench was an asshole and stuck on stupid. He stayed on all the wrong things, running up poker debts and paying on the bill as if it's layaway, smoking up guys K-2 and spit-a-rettes and not paying the bill. Wrench's thick-glasses wearing ass definitely had a very, very serious misconception. He actually thought he was the toughest among the toughies because he'd stabbed over 13 people. But little did he know, the young Mexican had been crazy since birth. He also was bred and trained to kill or be killed, since he was old enough to talk. Wrench's shot caller gave him the order of taking the 100 dollars that the Mexican offered to get his rightful cell back. But Wrench allowed one of his road dawgs to get in his ear to sell the cell to his homie for $150, so the cell could stay a black cell.

"Wrench, you know OG said take the Mexican's money, so we can squash the beef now," Bishops' homie advised. Wrench saw the fear in his homie's eyes, but he did not feel a mustard seed of fear.

"Bru, listen to your homie," an outsider said, "Take heed to what your OG said because it's not going to be y'all against them. It's gonna be all of them against all of us."

The brother's voice only added fuel to the fire. Wrench boldly stated, "I'm selling my cell to the Midwest guys for $150."

"Huh?" the Mexican breathed.

"You can huh. You can hear," Wrench popped slick.

Before he knew what was happening, the young Mexican had eased his bone crusher from his waist and shoved it into Wrench's neck, causing blood to squirt on his thick glasses lens and nappy hair. The rest of the Mexicans started stabbing the other brothers close to Wrench, and before long, the Mexicans and the Black's riot exploded to all the rec yard and in the housing units, because guys in the window saw this and even they had to take off on the Mexicans before they could do them.

Mr. Ben knew he'd do them before they do him. Mr. Ben's knife was the length of one's wrist to forearm, four inches wide. He stabbed to kill, not to hurt nor to paralyze. Mr. Ben downed a good ten, before he caught a blade in the side, and still managed to knock the Mexican's hand away from the weapon and penetrate his razor sharp blade into the guy's throat.

The officers and other staff raced around like a dog chasing its tail. They didn't know where to run to, because by the time their walkie-talkie was reporting the knife fight in one location, it began to report normal at other locations.

There were four units connected to building one, two, and building three, with a total of twelve units and four connected rec yards. Now, there were sixteen different places officers needed to be, and there weren't enough staff members. Once the staff secured a rec yard or housing unit by placing plastic cuffs on the inmates' wrists and ankles, they'd attract another location. There were sixteen hundred inmates on the compound; there would be a good number of a few hundred guys back to meet their makers. And another four or five hundred guys going to the outside hospital. The institution's medical would be able to fix and patch up the other couple hundred injured.

When the riot broke out on Shakur's yard, he looked

around for Sten, because by him being in a wheelchair, the opponent would see him as a very, very easy target.

"Oh, Allah," Shakur whispered, as the eight Mexicans began to formulate a circle around Sten X.

Sten's knuckles turned red and white, as he palmed the arms of his wheelchair with all his might. Sten X wanted to take the Mexicans to war so bad, that he wanted to cry. He overlooked the fact that he was outnumbered. He did not fear death. He only feared Allah. Sten X's old self-was fighting with his new self.

Demon's shadows rushed over his head, the devil himself stood behind Sten X with a puffed-up chest. Sten X had access to two bone crushers; he knew he could take two if not three with him. He wasn't going out alone, and definitely not without a fight. Sten X was going to prove that there wasn't anything easy nor sweet about him. They would think they had a lamb, and later realize they had an overgrown bear.

The shot caller among the group recognized Sten X and studied him, as they were approaching him. Shakur was racing towards them with all his might. One of the Mexicans caught a glimpse of Shakur out of the corner of his right eye. He notified his shot caller, and the leader commanded them not to move a muscle until he gave the order. Shakur and their shot caller had a good report, and they thought highly of Shakur, because Shakur even fueled a war of two different Mexican cars.

"What is this?" Shakur asked almost out of breath, once he reached arm's distance of the shot caller.

"The blacks wanna war, homie. So, we war," the shot caller said. He still had his knife drawn, as did his crew.

Shakur spread both of his hands, making it clear that he did not have a weapon. Nor was he there for war.

"I'm a Muslim. My brother in the wheelchair is a Muslim. We only fight if it's fi-si-bi-Allah," he paused to catch his breath before he continued, so the Mexican would understand and not overstand. "My friend, we don't fight unless it's the cause of Allah. I and my Muslim brothers don't want any problems with you guys." Shakur held up one finger. "If y'all don't harm one of my brothers, then there won't be no reason for this war to escalate."

"You people make no war with us?" the shot caller asked.

"No," Shakur said, "As long as you don't make no war with my Muslim brothers. You have my word on that."

"Your word," the Mexican shot caller said, knowing that once one gives their word, that's if they break the agreement, there were surely going to be a lot of dead bodies getting carried off the compound, just as sure as there's a God in heaven.

"Your word, amigo?" the shot caller asked again.

"Yes," Shakur nodded, "You have my word, but remember what I said. As long as nothing happens to my Muslim brothers, because if one is harmed, there wouldn't be room here for your car, and that's by Allah."

That was the day the Mexicans named Shakur "The Peacemaker." Shakur got with Wrench's shot caller and told him that a lot of good men, good soldiers had lost their lives and got tons of more time added to their sentence because he didn't properly handle the issue personally.

On these deadly and dangerous grounds, one can easily lose their life at the drop of a hat. 24/7, lives are in danger, and the crazy part about it is that one can lose their life over something that their homies did. One of the homies can do the dirty, and another homie in the car can and will reap the punishment. He can be the enemy on the street, but behind the USP walls, everyone from the same state must carry it as though they all came out of the same womb. Each one has another's life or freedom in one another's hands, whether he knows it or not. Here and here alone, one will have to want for his brother what he wants for himself.

**MEMORANDUM FOR All INMATES (USP)**
SUBJECT: Inmate Expectation During Emergencies

Recently, multiple inmates determined that they wanted to possess weapons and assault another inmate with a weapon in a situation in the recreation yard. While the staff were responding to the incident, the inmate population hindered staffs' response by failing to move out of the way, refusing to follow staff's direct orders, and failure to report to their assigned cells in a timely manner.

Safety of Staff and inmates is the top priority at U.S.P. Petty Rock. Steps will continue to be taken to ensure the safety and security of staff and inmates. Therefore, there is now ZERO TOLERANCE for inmates that are disrespectful or acting inappropriately while in the general population. If you decide to display such behavior, you will be removed from the general population and be subject to the inmate discipline process. In some cases, (i.e., possession of a weapon, groupings of inmates), the behavior will result in a referral to a Special Management Unit (SMU).

Continued evaluation of the operations at U.S.P. Petty Rock will be conducted prior to determining when the institution will open up for normal operations.

MEMORANDUM FOR INMATE POPULATION
UNITED STATES PENITENTIARY, PETTY ROCK (PHASE ONE)
SUBJECT: Outdoor Recreation

Due to the incidents that continue to occur throughout the institution, the softball field, football field, and handball court will be closed and the rotating recreation schedule previously used will be re-implemented.

The schedule will reflect one unit remaining in the housing unit pod area: and two units authorized outdoor recreation. The units and recreation yards will be rotated daily. Recreation activities will be based on Units. Upon closing of these areas, inmates will return to the yard assigned to their unit.

In addition, there are new "Out of Bounds" areas of the

Institution.

The re-opening of the Yards for recreational activities will be considered at a later date.

**MEMORANDUM FOR INMATE POPULATION**
UNITED STATES PENITENTIARY, PETTY ROCK

(PHASE TWO)
SUBJECT: Lock Down Reintegration Procedures

The purpose of this memorandum is to provide you with the Lock-Down Management Plan and Lock-Down Reintegration procedures. The Lock-Down Reintegration Procedures will be implemented for every Lock-Down situation in an effort to gradually resume normal operations of the institution as quickly as possible.

LOCK-DOWN MANAGEMENT PLAN

Friday

(Cells 1-16, 12:15 p.m. - 1:00 p.m.), (Cells 17-32, 1:00 p.m. - 1:45 p.m.),

(Cells 33-48, 1:45 p.m. - 2:30 p.m.), (Cells 49-64, 2:30 p.m. - 3:15 p.m.)

Televisions will be turned on from 9:00 a.m. to the 4 p.m. Stand-up Count. Inmates will be allowed to take showers, utilize phones, microwaves, etc.

Saturday

Total Lock Down. Televisions will be turned on from 8:00 a.m. - 8:00 p.m.

Solitary is a school
thou none care to learn
from it none instant
US better…

# CHAPTER 3

The SHU ain't nothing but another part of the jail, and when I tell you that this is a world of its' own, please believe it. Because back here, an officer doesn't get any respect, and if a female CO was wise, she definitely wouldn't want to work the Hole, unless it was by force and not by choice.

These guys would do anything and say all kinds of ungodly things. They gave the officers pure hell. They'd hope and pray for the CO they don't like to walk through so that they could give them a piece of their mind. Some inmates throw their body waste on the officers and find the situation very cute. Here is where a CO will get the blues and be called everything, but a child of God. And everything the inmate does to the officers, they'll be rewarded with a good laugh from the other inmates.

Freak-some sat in the middle of his bunk shooting generic Tylenol into the commode. Daily, he waited patiently for some staff member or CO to come by, so it'll make his day. If one doesn't have any patience, one will definitely learn some in the Hole, because the officers will never accommodate you on your time. It'll always be on their time.

The captain stopped by Freak-some's door. He cut the light on and looked around Freak-some's cell.

Freak-some got out of bed, and while walking up to the door, the Captain's voice went into motion as he said, “You got it made.”

“I don 't know how the fuck you come up with that,” Freak-some replied.

“Look at cha; you're still in a cell by yourself, you can get you a good piece of mind. Does your dick still get hard?”

“What you tryna do? What, you wanna suck some?” he

asked, loving every minute that the captain tried to pop slick, but was actually speaking Freak-some's language.

The Captain walked off, trying to get away before Freak-some went overboard and got carried away, which he was known to do. The guys on the Range were not satisfied with Freak-some's response.

They needed, wanted Freak-some to carry out an order what they're not brave enough to do or say: Roast the Captain to the fullest since he wanted to play.

"Freak-some, you got you one tryna GO, ain't it?" questioned cell 313. "Freak-some, that monkey tried you then," instigated cell 315.

"Man, that clown-ass nigga already know how I get down. He ain't brought no strong game plan to no weak ass nigga," Freak-some blurted.

"Already, huh man," cell 315 commented.

"He came to the right man with the right plan; I'd give his ass the deal of the century," Freak-some promised.

"What deal you got for him, Freak-some?" questioned cell 314.

"Homie, I know Captain tryna trade the cool-low for the swipe, I'll trade with him all day long. I can see him now, spread out on my bunk lookin' all pretty. I know he's trying to get that salad tossed. I'll carry out that order, everybody knows I'm crazy about that boy ponocha!"

"Freak-some will go coo-coo for Coco puffs!" joked cell 314.

"And you know it!" Freak-some confirmed. "Ain't no shame in my game."

"Give him a pass, Freak-some, he don't know any better," huffed cell 315.

"A pass my ass! Shit, them the best kind," Freak-some stated.

"When the Captain came through, I thought I saw a Puddy

cat, I did, I did, I did see a puddy cat," cell 313 teased, enjoying himself and showing Freak-some he's not the only one who can entertain the range.

The SHU Lieutenant walked over to Freak-some's door. "Bru, give the Captain a break for me? Will y'all please do that for me?" he pleaded, patting himself on the chest.

"Get your fat ass off of the range, fuckboy!" shouted cell 313, "Your dog ass needs roastin' too, but I'm givin' you a pass 'cause you put me in the mind of my favorite uncle."

"Give the Captain a break for what? That bitch, ho ass fuck nigga, it's too late in the game for that shit! I ain't even gonna lie to you, son." And with that, Freak-some went into his favorite mold, set out his demo casually. He started using the door as his personal set of drums, while he rapped through the steel door's speaker piece as if it were nothing other than a microphone.

"From age 8 to 80, blind crippled or crazy, I'm tryna go half on a ba-by."

"Oh, no, Freak-some, you burnt the fuck out." Cell 303 professed.

"I'm just doing what niggas do, when they don't know any better, or know right from wrong," Freak-some said, laughing. He's good for trying to justify his unlawful activities.

"Man, what's that Captain's name again?" Cell 316 asked.

"Call him Captain Ass," Freak-some answered.

"Freak-some, get off that damn door and stop making all that noise! You're giving me a headache!" the CO shouted.

"I'll jump right off this door and start banging on your ass! Come on up here, you beautiful, big boned motherfucker, I'll give you an ass-ache!" Freak-some replied, ready to keep the show in motion. "Put a long, curly, red wig on ya with some red or hot pink lipstick; you'll look as good as gold. You'd have Ru Paul beat! Ru Paul won't have shit on you, big guy. And I do mean nothing."

300 Range always stayed off the chain. Here's where most of the guys were on that “paid it, no mind” sheet because that's all they knew was doing and saying all the wrong things. The COs knew it was Freak-some's range, and he ran the show.

Now on the other hand, on Range 100, Big Dummy and Extra Stupid kept some propaganda going on. They were always doing something they didn't have any business doing. Holding the flap, breaking their water sprinkler, flooding their cell by putting their bedsheets in the toilet and using a blanket to stop the water from escaping under their door, until they're ready. They'd go out to rec and wouldn't cuff up, so they could be placed in their cell when the one-hour rec was completed. One of them would get on the cage and try to urinate on the COs. Sometimes, they'd take turns with their foolishness, but to them, it's having fun.

When the officers would be dealing with other guys on their range, they'd be hollering through the door,

“Go hard! Make 'em kill ya!”

“Man, DON 'T cuff up for them! You'll be weak if you do!”

“Homie, tell them to quit threatening you with them fake-ass orders!”

Big Dummy and Extra Stupid kept the COs catching hell. They knew when they worked in the SHU that it was going to be work, especially on their range. Today, Extra Stupid decided to let the officers take one of the cuffs off of his right wrist, and before he was able to take the left one off, Extra Stupid snatched his wrist back through the flap and stated,

“Get the FUCK away from my door! I ain't givin' you these cuffs; if you want them, you'll have to come in here and take them!”

“You a gangsta or a wanksta?” Big Dummy asked.

"Suit up!" Extra Stupid encouraged.

Sometimes, one must be careful about what they wish for because the CO did not hesitate to notify the Shift Lieutenant of these two bad boys' misconduct. Twenty minutes later, fifteen officers were standing beside their door wearing armor, as if they were on the street fighting a rioting crowd.

"You guys want to give me back my officer's cuffs?" asked the LT.

"I don't have no cuffs, Mr. Policeman," Big Dummy said in a childish voice, trying to be sarcastic.

"Are you going to hand over the cuffs?" the LT asked. He disregarded that these two stayed on some kind of N.W.A. time... "Fuck Tha Police."

"Lt. You a wanksta or a gangsta?" Big Dummy repeated.

The Lt. and the other officers could hear Ex-Stupid and Big Dummy kee-kee and haha about them. "Guys, if y'all don't hand over the cuffs, you know what's going to happen."

"What? What? What's gonna happen?" Ex-Stupid asked, though he already knew they were going to throw a couple of baby bombs into their cell. The loud explosion was going to have their ears stopped up, the tear gas was going to follow, then the officers were going to rush into their cell, handcuff them both, and escort them to the glass cube where it stayed cold. They'd be wearing paper white jumpsuits. The drill did not change; this was just a different day, is all.

"You guys giving up the cuffs, or do we have to go through this procedure?" asked the LT.

"You'll be weak if you don't," Ex-Stupid replied.

"We're going HARD in here, baby," Big Dummy said.

"If it ain't rough, then it ain't us," Ex-Stupid said.

"LT?" Big Dummy said.

"Yes? I'm listening."

"What y'all waiting on?" asked Extra Stupid.

"y'all scared?" asked Big Dummy.

These two foolish no-brainers never took the time out to think about the fact that they were putting themselves in harm's way, giving the officers a free probable cause to really hurt one of them. To Big Dummy and Extra-Stupid, this was all fun and games. Their highlight of the day. They loved the excitement.

The Hole had a steel shower, and these two idiots were using one of their green bed mats to create a door for the shower. As soon as the officers entered the small six-by-six cell, Big Dummy or Extra Stupid would pull the string that was tied to the water sprinkler, and the muddy black water would shower on the officers. Big Dummy and Extra Stupid had field days playing all kinds of deranged games on the SHU COs. The officers would get tired of causing them bodily harm before they would get tired of playing these unnecessary elementary games. Big Dummy and Ex-Stupid didn't have enough sense to know that the officers were trained on how to handle situations such as these. The whole officers soon learned to give Big Dummy and Ex-Stupid their props, as well as to respect their Gangsta. They knew the two knuckleheads wouldn't stop at nothing and refused to throw in the towel. So, the staff joined them, since they couldn't defeat them. They gave Ex-Stupid and Big Dummy extra food trays, extra rec hours, the phone, took them to the law library upon request. The no-brainers made the hole their Burger King; they had it their way.

***

U.S.P. Petty Rock was three months into their lockdown, due to multiple group stabbings and two inmates being murdered, when Zeek's counselor notified him that he'd be transferred to a lower level security camp before the week was out. Good thing he traded information with Shakur and Sten X the day the Unit Team put him in for transfer. Zeek

Bey phoned Shakur's mother to see how Shakur and Sten X were doing. She enlightened him that U.S.P. Petty Rock was back on Lockdown because of the Spanish and black riot. Zeek Bey prayed that his U.S.P. family was free of harm.

Now, with Zeek Bey being from behind the wall made him appreciate this spot. He didn't have to worry anymore about sitting at their assigned geographic table. One had to cell only with his car. He didn't have to trust any fake homies to have his back. Here, there was no shot-caller, and one doesn't have to deal with no homies period if he chose not to. There was no tension in the air, instead of every inmate having a knife or two. Here, there were probably ten knives total. Now, on the other hand, this place had no respect, these guys would say and do all type of disrespectful things which should have and would have been plenty to put many, many bodies in a body bag. Zeek Bey missed the blood shedding events and most of all the lockdowns because that is when he would get some good days of rest.

*"I finally escape the hell hole, now the people done put me into the circus,"* Zeek Bey thought. "*This place is full of mascots. These dudes play with that paper and pay on their bills as if it's layaway.*" He went to the Rec Yard. A group of youngsters was huddled up telling jokes about one another. There was an old man amongst the group. He was old enough to be their grandfather. His pants sagged, as well. "*Once a man, and twice a child.*" He pushed the corny institution-framed glasses a little farther up the bridge of his nose.

"You can't give, you can't think. I want you, fat boy since you said my breath stank," the old man said, pointing to the youngster that challenged him.

"Stay in your lane, old man," the youngster replied.

"All you niggas line up!" the old head stated. "Nigga, I'm an O.G.!"

"You're an O.F.," Jay Blast said, laughing.

"What's that mean?" the old head asked.

"Old Fool!" Gump said, laughing.

The first youngster that he challenged started rapping a song about the old fool.

"Every time you talk, you blowing shit in a nigga's face! Hobo, purchase you some Colgate and stop using the Fed's toothpaste! Holla bout you a gangsta, and that you real, If it wasn't for the chow hall, you wouldn't have a meal.

Hair Stink, Locker stink, body stink, bed stink, foot stink, the people know your raggedy ass mouth stank!

You were a junky; you awaken the dead when you fart,

You gave up on life, as well as on God.

You crippled, retarded, handicap, suicide patient,

You 61 years old in GED class, but I like the fact that you're trying to further your education

You think that selling Crack is better than getting a crazy check,

That PROVES that you're not playing with a full deck.

You holla bout you still gonna sell Crack, and rob

You're an old dog still chase its tail, and I see you ain't tired of doing the devil job.

You're the skunk king…

In jail, living out your American Dream."

Zeek Bey went to the law library to get away from the foolishness. As soon as he entered the library, he saw two guys sitting at the back table arguing over the Bible. The brother hauled off and slapped the man that was old enough to be his father. The elder man demonstrated what the Bible said one should do, he turned the other cheek toward the prey and asked did he want to slap the other cheek. The brother didn't know how to respond to such conduct, so he tucked his tail and fled. And he became the joke of the compound. His guilty conscious later asked the elder for forgiveness.

The elder told him the apology was not accepted, because if one is genuinely the Child of God, and in public, one proclaimed to be the Lord's Loyal Servant, this event should not have taken place.

Zeek Bey decided he'd witnessed enough of this comic show for one day. He went back to his cell, where he knew he could get some peace, because his celly stayed gone until 8 p.m. recall. The more people change, the less they have in common with most people.

Responsibility to awaken others…

Knowledge passed on is living
wisdom, and power is in that.

# CHAPTER 4

Six months after lockdown, Shakur pushed Sten X towards the chow hall. The group of guys was discussing the institution meal.

“Boy, they're serving that swine!”

“Shit, I'm just mad the swine don't get as big as an elephant.”

“Playa, I grew up on that willy. I'll eat it from the rooter to the tooter.”

“That was slave food in the days.”

Shakur stopped the wheelchair so that the guys could put some distance between them. He and Sten X weren't going to show anyway. They were getting some fresh air and stretching their legs. Five brothers were heading in Shakur and Sten X's direction. Shakur shared his plan with them.

“Brothers, we're going to have a meeting every Tuesday in the chapel at the 6:30 move. We need brothers with a voice to be present so that we can start some kind of unity.”

“Brother Shakur, I would like to support your cause, but I work six days a week and overtime most of the time,” Dan said.

“You take your ass out there to that plantation. You should be able to give Brother Shakur one hour of your time. We all need to speak positive for food for thought,” stated Nard.

“I'll be there, Brother Shakur,” Big Buck said, “Cause I got something serious that these youngsters need to hear, before they get themselves killed or in a world of trouble. These youngster's overlooking at utilizing this prison term as a wakeup call to better themselves for society. They stay on a suicidal mission, as if they're really out for a death wish. They're making it harder for the prison system to accomplish their goal and policy of keeping the place free of violence. Not every guard is safe in prison, let alone the inmates. Always senseless, brutal murders are carried out. Becoming a model prisoner is surely not on some of these young buck's agendas."

"I strongly believe that the measure of a man is how he responds to adversity. Once some guys get sentenced to these long bids, they give up humanity, forcing some guards to believe that U.S.P.s are filled with society's ultimate losers. And by them being on the same danger grounds are forcing them to hold fast to their negative thinking and negative way of life. They refuse to let go of the unlawful mentality that got them in this situation. They still get trapped into trying to prove they're hard by carrying out unnecessary activities. This such conduct is a sickness. They have so much to prove to their homies, to the compound, that they are totally X'ing out their kids and loved ones," Wyzell said. He was willing and ready to say more. Once he started teaching and sharing the knowledge, he didn't know how to stop.

Shakur smiled because this is what he needed. He needed all the old heads to speak to the people, to speaks to their cars, to their homies, and once he was able to get everyone on one accord, him and Sten X would be able to sing Frankie Beverly's song, *We Are One.*

"The Youngsters don't have any integrity about themselves, they have a character disorder," Lil Mo stated.

Frank stood back long enough, but now, he decided to speak. "Sometimes, before we can prejudge someone, you have to know them and walk a mile in their shoes."

After Lil Mo took a couple of swallows of coffee, he was

ready to speak again. "Sometimes, when you're standing in a circle, looking at the circle, you do not see the circle, so you need somebody outside of the circle to tell you what the circle looks like." He paused to look into each individual's face, to see if he had lost anyone with his circle metaphor, "Meaning a person does not see their own faults. Their mind is the limit."

The compound officer walked closely by the huddle to hear hustle and so that everyone would hear his voice. "Speaking of circles, you guys have to keep it moving. I have been watching y'all, and y'all have been huddled up over here for almost 35 minutes," he said politely and in a professional manner.

"We're moving, Fat Jesus," one of the guys addressed the officer. He always told the CO that he looked like a fat Jesus with sunglasses. Every time he would see the officer, he would always call him 'Fat Jesus'.

A youngster walked by and saw his homie eating a pork chop sandwich. "Break bread as Jesus said!"

His homie shot Shakur a wink and addressed his homie's slick comment, "God can't keep saving you. You need to holler at the Lord and ask him to turn you away from your wicked ways. You can't depend on the B.O.P. if that's what you're looking for. You're putting checks in their pockets," he added the last sentence, because of Fat Jesus' presence.

"All we can do is pray for them," said Big Buck.

"We are our brothers' keepers," Sten X reminded him, "That's our duty since we are all the children of God."

"Everyone has a calling, brothers," Shakur stated, looking around making sure that their private circle all agreed, before he continued, "Everyone needs to do their duty. We're all only on the Earth for a temporary consignment. Many are called, but only a few are chosen."

"God gives everybody an opportunity," Big Buck said.

"I agree Buck," Frank agreed, while rubbing his bald head and running his right hand over his well-groomed, snow-white beard, "That's a fact."

Shakur looked over to the old head named Zeke. "Zeke, out of respect, what you think about our unity?"

"It would be a beautiful thing. A beautiful demonstration, Brother Shakur," Zeke exhaled out, "But in today's time, our young people have become so foolishly blinded to think that who we are, and what we are has nothing to do with the next person. That what we say and what we do has no effect on others. This line of thinking is what makes us selfish, conceited, inconsiderate of others, and stubborn. A wise man, named Elihu, once said, no man lives unto himself, for every living thing is bound by invisible cords to every other living thing. Blessed are the pure of heart, for they will love and demand love in return. They will not do to other men what they would not have other men do unto them. We always speak about Unity amongst each other, but if one doesn't understand the unity and how it has been strategically formulated into the course of nature by the creator, then there is no way an individual can conceive how Unity is even possible."

---

After Big Ro finished his shower, he slipped into a purple robe and headed straight to his bar. Big Ro needed a drink, and the strong liquor began to put his body to ease, but not to tamper with his mind. Sten X had been pretty heavy on his mind lately. Some days, he would be passing a lot of time thinking what Sten would've done.

"This" or "That."

Big Ro washed down the small glass of Ace of Spade and immediately refilled it. He again emptied the glass in one giant swallow. Big Ro had been procrastinating and trying his best to resist watching the video of Sten X's downfall. Big Ro had hidden cameras in the front and back tags of his

Benz and Rolls Royce, which was for the purpose of seeing if one of his prey or opponents wanted to try anything stupid. Now, he was glad to have the cameras. They had served their purpose.

Big Ro finally reached the destination of his movie theater. He selected to sit on the couch instead of in the recliner chair. He gripped the cream-colored, soft, leather couch pillow.

"Sten."

"Sten."

"Sten."

"Oh God, Sten," he mumbled while collecting the remote to the 82-inch flat screen that was mounted on the wall before him. Within normal seconds, tech screen came to life after his thumb assaulted the remote control button. Big Ro was back into the past, yes, revisiting down memory lane, which he had done on several occasions against his will, only to feed his conscience. It always crushed his heart and damaged his spirit, witnessing Sten X fall victim to the prey.

Even though Sten had done a lot of Big Ro's dirty work, he didn't look at Sten as his do-boy, flunky, or hitman. Big Ro loved young Sten as if he was his biological son. Yes, as his flesh and blood. He couldn't talk young Sten out of his lifestyle, so Big Ro had paid him top dollar and a lot of times, he did things for Sten when he did not have an assignment for him. Ro would've given one arm and both of his legs to have Sten a free man.

"POW."

"POW."

"POW."

"POW."

All was heard as the screen displayed the Detective and Sten exchanging gunfire.

"One down and only one more to go," Big Ro said, as if he'd seen this video before, or maybe he was trying to talk things into existence.

Sten continued to jog backward as the gunplay continued. The detective had feared for his life, thinking he too would be on the front page of the newspaper like his partner, lying dead as a doorknob in his own pool of blood. Then one mistake needed unfolded, and the detective took full advantage of it as Sten's pants began to slip and slide down his small waist. The two-size-too-big pants weren't in Sten's favor, because this time, they worked against him. His cool pretty boy swagger made him a complete target, caused him to be converted from the predator to the victim. As Sten lowered both pistols trying to pull up his pants, the detective capitalized off of Sten's *Mr. no-no*. The Detective began assaulting the trigger as every round exploded into Sten's body. The detective carried on as though he had a grudge with his weapon, then with Sten, as he greeted, "Die, motherfucker, die." His bullets used Sten as target practice. The detective's deceased partner continued to flash before his eyes, as Sten X was falling to the pavement. Once Sten's body connected with the ground and was spread out, looking dead, the Detective wasted no time racing over to Sten's body and kicking the other pistol from Sten's loose grip. In the detective's mind, Sten was dead, because no one could still be breathing after fifteen shots to the body, but the detective wanted to put some insurance on it to make sure Sten didn't return from death or escape his deathbed. He knelt beside Sten's head, disregarding the sound of sirens in the backgrounds, disregarding the cars speeding towards his back, and growled, "You got-damn nigga," as he pressed the barrel to Sten's head and pulled the trigger. This is what made the detective feel more at ease with himself. Tears began to run down Big Ro's face. He never cried behind one single killing that he'd witnessed, but this one stroked and touched a nerve, a big nerve. Big Ro's eyes began to get smaller, as he continued watching the screen and witnessed himself rushing out of the back of his Benz and racing to

Sten's motionless body. He squeezed Sten's hand, and in his mind all he saw was death, smelled death, and tasted death as he touched death. Big Ro reached under his shirt, locking his finger on the trigger of the 9mm. He wanted to give the detective the same punishment as a reward. The police car's loud siren came to a complete halt several feet away from him. As Big Ro heard the tires cry out from the breaks, he could also smell the oil drip and drop from the leaky motor.

Police crowded among them.

"Did you get him?" One officer asked the detective.

"Yes," the detective said with pride, "he's dead."

"Good job," the police officer said, patting the detective on the back. "Good work."

Big Ro blinked his eyes a couple of times as he studied the detective's face on the screen, and four of his five senses began to interact with death.

He saw death. Smelled death. Touched death. And tasted death.

---

Sten's mother vacuumed the living room floor as she listened to R. Kelly's song, *Step*.

She also danced around with the vacuum, which she called her exercise. The only time R&B music was played was on the days she vacuumed because all she listened to was the gospel. She had a beautiful voice. She could and would sing some gospel songs better than the artists. Now, the song was *The Electric Slide* and *The Chow Chow*. Sten's mother would give her vacuum cleaner a run for its money. She promised to shake off a few pounds. Once the vacuum was placed back into the closet, her house phone began to ring. She answered on the first ring, "Hello?"

"How are you doing, Ms. Peabody?"

"I'm okay, and how about yourself, sir?"

Sten's mother recognized Big Ro's voice off the drabbler

and wondered to herself why he was calling her. The last time he was over at her house, she gave him all the information needed, so he would be able to send Sten the monthly allowance personally.

"I know you're probably wondering why I'm calling you."

"Yes," Sten's mother said, and answered, "I know it's concerning my only child."

"Yes," Big Ro stated, "And Ms. Peabody, it's very important to me that you know I love Sten as my son as well."

"That's good to learn, Mr. Ro."

"When Sten calls you tonight, would you please tell him to give me a call? I feel the need to hear my son's voice today, as well."

"Yes, I can do that for you, sir," Sten's mother said, as a few tears began to float down her face freely. She thought she was the only one that loved Sten. "Mr. Ro, it would be a pleasure."

"Ms. Peabody, you have a blessed night, and I sincerely apologize for the intrusion."

She heard the dragging in Big Ro's voice and knew there was some alcohol in his system, and counted her blessings that he'd had the courage to say the words tonight.

"Sir, you have an even more blissful night. And Mr. Ro, there's nothing for you to apologize for."

"Good night, Ms. Peabody."

"Good night, sir," Sten's mother said, and dropped to her knees. "Oh Lord, Thank You for being a merciful Lord. Thank you for allowing my child to repent. I know Sten's not in the place where he wants to be, but he's in a safe place to be. Thank you for not taking my child out of my life for good. Continue to clean his heart, Lord. Sten's not the man he used to be; all praises belong to you. God, please bless my son, so he'll be able to be a blessing to others. Thank you, precious Lord, for saving my son, I know you have not finished working with him. Lord, keep your words and name in his mind, mouth, and heart." Sten's mother could not and would not stop thanking and praising the Lord for the extraordinary job that was done to Sten. Sten's mother knew she couldn't stop his wrongdoing, but she was wise enough to pray concerning all of her son's ugly situations. She put Sten in the hands of the Lord. The Lord answered her prayers.

By renewing your mind, it brings you to rare exposure of knowledge, wisdom, and understanding that can change the way we think, by revealing a truth of which we are unaware, renewing our minds firmly molds our lives into a network of principles and rules for the guidance of an appraisal of our conduct. In the least, we are being fused with morality; conscious efforts to do what is right in accordance with our teachings. We are fast becoming a working, thinking, planning group of people with common goals that unite us around an ideological concept of ourselves (society).

Others before us have brought their desires and visions to the doorsteps of reality. Whether we do so as well and cross the threshold of achievement depends entirely on one person, the one whom each of us see in the mirror.

Ignorance is no longer an adequate excuse for failure! Why? Because virtually all limitations are self-imposed! You will soon realize that you, the individual, are a minute expression of the creator of all things, and as such, you have no limitations except those accepted in your mind. Every man and woman has within himself or herself a sleeping giant. No one needs to be less than he or she is!

There rests within each of us the power to become great in their own way. Finding one's true self is the beginning of success, simple as it sounds, many travels through life without the vaguest notion of their true selves and the meaning of life. There are ingredients, like pieces of a puzzle, waiting to be placed by you into one breathtaking work of art. This process can and must be in the final analysis to overcome ignorance. This can only be accomplished if you remain receptive and teachable of the gifts handed down from God for us to build from, and it is vital for us to teach others the importance of the building of their prosperity. (The price of ignorance, the cost of an education.)

# CHAPTER 5

Chase stood in his cell window, watching the clock. For some strange reason, he'd become accustomed to watching the clock.

"We got work, we got work, we got work!" the announcer announced through his cell door, letting it be known that a prisoner was coming.

"Yo, CO, you need to get up off ya fat ass and make some rounds, cause I need my toilet flushed!" someone shouted.

The toilet had to be flushed from the outside. It was sad and bad that the COs capitalized on that and used it to their advantage. If someone talked crazy to the officer or did something they didn't like, they'd take their own sweet time with the accommodation. The COs were going to dish out punishment in every way that he or she possibly could and get away with it. They were the judge, jury, and executioners. Once someone was under their roof, they'd make the rules as well as break the rules. One was in a 'no win' situation and yet refused to throw in the towel, because they fight battles that were impossible to win since the deck was stacked against them before they started.

The staff lied for other staff members. They weren't going to take the side of a prisoner against their co-worker. They could witness the event and even know the prisoner was right. The system trailed them that way.

Chase's mind went to the question his little brother had asked him a while back, when he didn't give an answer, because he didn't have an answer. Now, while he was sitting in his cell all alone, his mind could produce many answers, because all he could do was think. His mind wasn't polluted with the weed, jailhouse liquor, and rap music. When he was a free man, all that he saw, had, and delivered was the wrong answers, but now, with God in his life, all he saw, carried, and delivered were the right answers.

"What good does it do a man to lose the world and regain his soul?" his brother had asked him.

Chase altered the sentence, "What good it does a man to lose the world and gain his soul?" Chase now answered the question out loud and smiled to himself, because each word that rolled off his tongue and escaped from his lips sounded mighty beautiful to his ears.

Chase's conscious refused to be content with just that answer now that his mind had a mind of its' own and felt the extreme need of a revelation. Once one tried to gain the world, it was mandatory that the scale became unbalanced, and surely everything in life has to balance out equally. And one can rest assured that while on this mission, chasing the delusion, Satan, the devil, was definitely going to be one's chief. And it never ever fails. The devil loans the people all these luxuries, gifts, toys, women, and the same way he gave it to the people, he'd come back and take it back from the people. He made one a wolf, and when he got tired of one, he'd feed one back to the wolves. The devil comes to deceive, kill, steal, and destroy. Yes, rob one of their future and forces one against their own will to abandon their blessings from God secretly.

God said, "If you love me, if you worship me, and obey my commands, then I shall give you an abundance of life."

"See, when the devil destroys you, robs, and rapes you of the wealth that you inherit from him and through him, he'll feed you off to the prison system or the graveyard, and he'll sit back and laugh at you. The world will forget about you; you will no longer exist."

God will give you tenfold of what the devil had given, and in return, all God wants is for you to worship him and follow his commands, and not be ashamed to give testimony. God is a good God all the time. God is a mysterious God. God is also the best of planners. There's no limit to what the almighty powerful Lord can do. We're in need of God; God is not in need of us. You worship God, and you're promised to be rewarded.

Chase's brain forced his body to drop down into praying position immediately, and his tongue began to carry on as his weapon.

"Lord, I'd like to thank you for waking me up this morning, as well as for allowing me to be in my right frame of mind. I want to thank you for allowing me to see, and most of all I'd like to thank you for allowing me to be amongst the land of the living. Lord, you spared my life, for what reason I do not know. Lord, please give me the signs and your symbols as well as guide me to be pleasing to you. Now, I want to become your soldier; I want to show you, prove to you that I am worthy of your praise and blessings. God, tame my tongue and reprogram my mind. Purify my body. Strengthen my weak flesh. Armor me with your way of life. Make me into the servant that you need me to be. Amen."

***

Two hours later, the CO made rounds, flushing the people's toilets upon request. The other guys, who were waiting to get their toilet flushed that had fallen asleep were shit out of luck.

Chase was standing by the door when the CO tried to sneak past his cell. The CO hoped and wished that Chase was asleep as well, so he could punish him too by not flushing his toilet, so he'd have to smell the fluids of his body waste.

"Man, why you are always standing by the door?" the CO

asked Chase.

"I will be watching the clock."

"Watching the clock?" the CO repeated Chase's answer because he had never heard that answer before. That would be a first and a last.

"And I will be making sure you don't tiptoe past my cell like you do everybody."

"That's because of their mouth," the CO said, with a small laugh.

"Treat others like you would like to be treated," Chase said, looking the CO in his eyes. "Bru, you wouldn't want your kids, brothers, or nephews to be mistreated."

"I feel that," the CO nodded, "When you're right, you right." Now, the CO called himself kicking the bo-bo with Chase like he did with other prisoners, using them to assist him with completing his eight-hour shift, so the day would fly by. "They fed y'all that same cut up chicken last night, then they turned back around and fed it to y'all again today as the lunch meal. They got so many of y'all locked up; now, they can't afford to feed you. They already feed y'all chicken two or three times a week."

"I have learned to be thankful for any meal that I get through the slot," Chase politely knocked on the steel flap that was designed for meals to be passed through. "Some people in other countries, third world countries, don't even have that."

"I can say amen to that," the CO agreed with another nod.

"A man in my position, I have learned to count my blessings, and I have asked the Lord to be my provider. I don't need everything the world has to offer. Now, I'm content with the blessings that I get from God."

"God bless you two times," the CO said to Chase, before walking off.

"And God bless you ten times," Chase returned, as well as upgraded the blessing.

The CO started singing, My God is AWESOME ..." but

by the time he made it back down the stairs, he was back on joke time. “If I was locked in one of the cells like Y'all for 23 straight, 24 hours on weekends and holidays, I would be like big playa up there,” the CO paused to point towards Chase's cell. “I would be solo! I'd refuse to take a celly, cause we wouldn't be able to flush the toilet when we want to. I ain't finna sit around in a funky cell and smell doo-doo or boo-boo all day until somebody came around to flush the toilet!” The CO shook his head from left to right, making a sad face, being silly. “It wouldn't be me. It's not gonna happen.”

“Man, you tryin' to serve two masters,” Chase mumbled. “It's not gonna happen. It's not gonna be me.”

When one does tic for tac… One incorporates that individual characterize.

# CHAPTER 6

## THE CULTURAL ENLIGHTENMENT SUMMIT

The Cultural Enlightenment Summit will discuss, plan, and orchestrate ways to comprehensively solve the ills of society's complex human rights issues.

Monthly, the summit will have a candid dialogue with all religious communities, races, and affiliations concerning important issues such as: Unity, Improving the Family, and Reprogramming the Mind to break away from prejudicial thought, to embrace individuals as human beings.

The Summit will encourage the religious communities, races, and affiliations to unite to find real solutions to the real problems facing all of humanity.

Religion is supposed to be *the foundation of life*. Without it, we are conformed to our lower selves, but division also conforms us. We must erase the line, cross the bridges, and see each other from a human perspective.

The dialogue will take place on Monday. All positive thinkers are welcome.

Shakur asked these wise brothers to be present the first day, because he needed to be sure they all were on the same page. These six guys and himself would be the seven wise ones, so they could counsel their car as well as other guys until they all became as one. Shakur had talked with each of these knowledgeable brothers one-on-one whenever the opportunity was presented. During their days on the rec yard, him and R. Nalls El would go to show together. They always spent time together. He would always joke with Shakur about their fighting record being seven million and zero.

R. Nalls El's private joke meant him, and Allah (God)

never lost a battle.

"Mo, you have something that you would like to share with the other brothers before we begin?" Shakur addressed R. Nalls El.

R. Nalls El stood and greeted, "Peace and love, my brothers."

Everyone greeted the same greeting as he held up one of his flyers. R. Nalls El continued, "I'm going to give every one of you brothers a flyer. Would you please put it on the board in your Unit for me?" After he finished passing out the sheets, Shakur gave everyone the chance to read over the paper.

**ATTENTION!!!**

THE VOICE OF THE PROPHET is calling out to all Nationalized Moors and Conscious Men that they aid in the mission to uplift themselves and fallen humanity.

Here at Petty Rock, we are all experiencing abnormal conditions that are desperately in need of instructions that will help guide us on this treacherous path. It will be by adhering to the wisdom handed down to us by our forefathers that we will place ourselves in good grace with each other, but also with the one true creator of the Universe.

We all should have the same mission: To Grow and Mature, mentally and spiritually, gain discipline and inner strength, and to return back to our loved ones whole - Unbroken by the influence of the ignorance that we see demonstrated by those who aren't concerned with principles and family values.

**COME ALL!!**

There should be nothing more important than self-preservation and spiritual elevation. A group of people not guided are people divided! Unleash yourselves from the attachments of prison politics and relink yourselves with the characteristics and studies that would make your father, mother, children, and wives proud.

An hour and half, once a week of positivity can make a lot of difference in your life. (Especially with so much negativity around.)

**WHEN:** Friday at 5:00 p.m., first Religious Move (Beginning Next month, time will change to 6:00 p.m. Religious Move.)

**WHERE:** Main Chapel

WE ACKNOWLEDGE ALL THE TRUE AND DIVINE TEACHINGS OF JESUS, MOHAMMED, BUDDAH, CONFUCIOUS, ETC.

Once everyone gave Shakur their undivided attention, he began.

"Beacon - the light that gives guidance. The light that gives guidance to help one find a way during the path of following darkness.

"Every day is supposed to be a learning experience that helps direct the course we take during the passage of our lives. Often, we take little or no heed to the events that transpire around us, that would otherwise provide us direction in the paths we choose to take.

"However, short or long the remainder of our life may be, our experiences that have occurred and will continue to occur, daily will be the beacon that will guide our conduct and behavior in the dealings with our fellow man. However, as we are wise enough to know, sometimes, our young brothers do lots of things out of confusion, frustration, and out of anger."

Shakur paused and looked over to Frank, "Frank, would you please share with me and the other brothers the parable of the starfish?"

"Brother Shakur, it would be my pleasure," Frank said, and he began.

*Once upon a time, there was a wise man who used to go to the ocean to do his writing. He had a habit of walking on the beach before doing his work. One day he was walking along the shore, and as he looked down the beach, he saw a human figure moving like they were performing a dance. He smiled to himself to think that someone would dance to the day. So, he began to walk faster, to catch up. As he got closer, he saw that it was a young man, and the young man wasn't dancing, but instead was reaching down to the shore, picking up something, and very gently throwing it into the ocean. As he got closer, he called out, "Good morning! What are you doing?"*

*The young man paused, looked up, and replied, "Throwing Starfish in the ocean."*

*"I guess I should have asked, but why are you throwing starfish in the ocean?" the wise man requested because he'd witnessed the young man throw several into the ocean, before he approached him out of curiosity.*

*"The sun is up and the tide is going out, and if I don't throw them in, they'll die!" the young man replied.*

*"But young man, don't you realize that there are miles of beach and starfish all along it? You can't possibly make a difference!"*

*The young man listened politely, then bent down, picked up another starfish, and threw it into the sea, past the breaking waves, and said, "It made a difference for that one."*

After he finished, Frank looked into each brother's eyes

and said, “One person can make a positive difference,” and he politely sat back down.

“A tool of expression,” Shakur began as he took back over the conversation. “We lack motivation; we lack role models. We are the future, and what we do will affect the future. I'm one of the kids that didn't have a father there, but my heavenly father was always there. We are blessed, and we are a blessing to others, little do we know.” He continued as he walked from behind the desk and sat on top of it.

“Identity comes not from what rolls off the tongue, but from how one performs. Separate the real from the fake. How many stand-up guys can take their weight? The majority hide behind that mask, like a robbery, but only God can judge. But we ARE able to judge by one’s actions. I just want better for the youth, better for the fallen soldier’s seeds, and most of all, to better our condition as a whole. Life is just one giant stage, what's inside will surface, and that is how we will all be judged. My beloved brothers, it's not how one begins the race, but how one ends the race,” Shakur said and noticed the congested look on Sten X's face. “Sten X, you look as though you have something to say. Bru, by all means, release your burden.”

Sten X began. “We're in a shallow grave. People know about it, they're just walking over us. They've left us for dead. The things people glorified, they should be ashamed of. Like how we exploit our women on TV, and these studio gangstas rappin' about the lifestyle some people had to go through to get out of and better their situation.

“The glory and shame are truly misplaced, that we see in our society. We allowed drugs and alcohol to be put into our community. We're tearing down the same community our parents came up in.”

“Walking around with a knife every day... this is something that I did not want to do, because I had to do it! Education is key. With education, you can unlock any door.

Out of all of our so-called Great Leaders, Obama showed us; the most important is that education is the key. Don't think he's sitting there because of the color of his skin. Put all your effort into education. Put education over your sport. They can take that ball from you, but they can't take that knowledge from you."

"There is so much foolishness on the compound. They think they can't do anything else! That's what builds the character of a man, by the obstacles. God may set up ten roads that lead to the same place, but all of them are going to have different obstacles that build different folds of man. If you can go there without falling in the cracks and propaganda, you can endure anything. This place is only a learning experience. A better person, or a better criminal?"

Immediately after Sten X sat back down, Young Rico raised his right hand.

"Speak, little brother," Shakur instructed him.

"What foundations are they staying on? They are going to give you the riches of that foundation. They're supposed to be standing on the foundation. Ask them what example they're giving to support what they say that they are standing on. The foundation of what they say they're standing on, they are not living it, there is nothing in their daily lives or their actions to support what they say they are standing on. They believe that the riches that they go through are their support, but that is not true. You can tell someone about the things that they do, that doesn't say that they're not who they say they are, it just shows you who they are, because they can say one thing, but their actions will support and say another. If you're standing on something, your work will show the resolves of that, what you are standing on." Young Rico made his message powerful and super sweet, so no one would have any problems with digesting it. Then, Buck raise his right hand, "Unk, speak," Shakur said.

"The Nation saw that we fit the description of the Lost

sheep in the Bible and Qu'ran, meaning that we are not a physical sheep but a mental one. We are easily led away like the sheep. We are lost mentally, spiritually, and socially. We're so lost that we despise our doctors through propaganda and manipulation, we destroy one another," Big Buck enlightened, and added, "Through the history of man, the longest periods of peace have come after war. Men know what *beef* is, it's meat. It comes from a cow. But all this unnecessary beefing and senseless wars have to stop. Very few people know what squash is. It's a vegetable, or is it a fruit? Or something in between. But now all of us in this room know that the beef is squashed. By the grace of God, we are able to see the best in our young people, while the administration could only see the worst in them."

Shakur looked in Zeke's direction. "Brother Zeke, what's on your mind, O.G."

Zeke stood and began. "I know that the majority of us might have said or thought, or probably have even heard someone say, 'Man, prison discriminates just against us.' But have you taken the time out to analyze your question? Sometimes we need to try being completely honest with ourselves. Sometimes, one can set themselves up for failure unintentionally. Most guys in prison don't have a high school diploma or GED and run around like a chicken with his head cut off. Education is the key, my people. Without education, we set ourselves up for the penitentiary. If you don't know much, then you don't do much. Let's stop setting ourselves up for failure. We don't stop guiding; we don't stop teaching, we don't stop caring, because some people's comprehension process may take longer than others.

"I thank God every day for keeping us all amongst the land of the living. We may fall short of the glory, but we're blessed to see another day. May God continue to use us to his glory. Because God knows us better than we know ourselves. I pray that our father in heaven stops allowing our young people to get caught up among this crazy world. And make them the person that he wants them - and us - the person that he needs us to be, and gives us some peace. I also thank God for keeping us out of harm's and danger's way. My brothers, our destiny is too important to give up for anything. This is not the time to lose our focus. We have lots of work to do for the Lord.

God gives his hardest battle to his best soldiers."

Big Buck cut in and said, "Amen, Brother. I'm a living witness."

Zeke continued, "The only person who can hurt you is you. When one tries to change, one is battling against oneself. The old you is fighting against the new you."

"Preach, Brother Zeke, Teach, Brother Zeke," encouraged Big Buck, thinking that Zeke was taking the words right out of his mouth.

Zeke continued, "Love, truth, justice, freedom, and peace. If people apply it to their lives, they'll get something good."

"That's the truth *OG*," R. Nalls El stated.

Zeke started back speaking, "To have the knowledge and not share it would surely be an injustice. So brothers, I beg you, please don't be like a tree without roots. People without knowledge can't grow. Jesus said 'Do the work of me, and the work of our father. Our God Allah. What I have done, all men can do, and what I am, all men shall be. Our youth must know that God wouldn't put anything on them that they can't bear! God wishes for no man to perish. The devil was the strongest angel God created. The people have to trust in God, and allow God along the way to direct their step. The devil is a very great manipulator, the greatest debater in the Universe. These prisons have done some people some good, some have found wisdom."

"I pray three times a day, so I can stay in spirit with God," Big Buck said. "They see me with the Bible, they say I'm crazy, but if I was out there smoking crack or deep in sins, they'd pat me on my back."

Zeke picked back up, "It's not what a man takes in his body, but what he perceives out of his mouth. They tell you that in the Bible. I pray to matter, to make a difference, to have an impact. Here, one can make a huge imprint. Our youth has to learn to do unto others as though they would want to be done to them. They can take control of their journey and make it legendary. Our youngsters waste energy. So many misguided young men! They constantly fed one another with worse information; they need to change the way they think and wake up with a better attitude. They have not, cause they have asked not.

"You're going to meet all different kinds of people from all different kinds of works of life. Few and far between will be people with a sincere quality. Speaking of qualities, they come few and far between and meeting one will become rare in time. It will be thousands of years before you meet one that will come and be real. Dealing with you with no strings attached, that will be straight up and real with you. Then it will take a lifetime to meet one that will come and be sincere with any and everything that they will show and give you. If you would allow them to pour the wisdom, knowledge, and understanding of life in your head but before you can conceive of these things, you have to be able to recognize these rare individuals when, or if, they ever come into your lifetime. We're so caught up in foolishness and trickery that we are too blind to recognize these individuals for who they truly are. So, we'll miss out on the messages, advice, and guidance they can give us."

GOD defines LOVE as

Chastity,<br>
Sacrifice,<br>
Obedience,<br>
Patience,

Long-Suffering,
Forgiveness...
Without that, you will have

**AFFLICTION**.

# CHAPTER 7

Shakur's cousin, Reese, paced around his living room looking extra stupid. All Shakur ever done was try to make sure he ate off of his plate. Sometimes Shakur would give him weapons for free. Reese's slimy and grimy butt would sometimes lie to Shakur, that he had to run off and leave the weapons, because the police were chasing drug dealers off the block and out of the projects. Shakur always told him, he could always get some more weapons and that he'd do the right thing because he didn't want him in prison. Shakur would often joke that prison wasn't even for the birds, he wouldn't even wish it on his worst enemy.

Reese heard through the grapevine that the two detectives, he'd set Shakur up with, had finally gotten indicted for selling the weapons from the evidence room. They'd be putting the weapons back on the streets, back into the young African Americans' hands. The best customers were the gang bangers. Reese had proof; he'd read and re-read the article.

"Y'all slick devils finally got caught up," he said, as he palmed the newspaper. "Shakur, big bruh, I'm sorry. Now, these devils caught you; two wrongs don't equal no right. They gave you 65-years for the guns, and you haven't killed anybody."

Reese called Shakur's mother and asked her to please relay the message to Shakur before the week was out. He said he would write Shakur and send him the clipping out of the newspaper, and he would speak on Shakur's behalf in court because he had lots and lots of dirt on the two detectives. They'd done plenty of business together. Reese sold a few thousand weapons for them, and most of the time, they didn't show him any love. They overlooked the fact that if Reese had snitched on his first cousin, what did he care about snitching on them?

"I oughta kill ya."
"Once a snitch, always a snitch."

"What would keep you from snitching on us?"

Reese revisited some of the cruel things they would say to him. Actually, they treated him like the sellout that he was.

Reese used his right sleeve to wipe the runny snot from his nose. "Shakur, I got you to put in there. I'm going to help get you out. God is my witness." Reese began to write down data and transactions that he'd done for the dirty detectives. Now he could care less if they incriminate him for his role, but by law, he'll remain a free man, because the authority was the bosses, and bosses make and break the rules.

---

Shakur sat on the bench in front of the law library, his mind heavily occupied with his first cousin, Reese. He no longer held Reese accountable for his incarcerations. If Reese didn't set him up, he could have lost his life during a shoot-out with the law enforcer, if they'd caught him on better grounds. A made up mind is the strongest thing in the Universe. Shakur said if anyone tried to jack him for his weapons, they would have to kill him to get them. He only saw a one-way road, and the end of the tunnel was death. He was wise enough to know a coin had two sides, but Shakur only mentally saw it as one-sided. Narrow-minded, and single-minded.

A 5' 9" brother weighing 170 pounds started walking towards Shakur. Shakur smiled as he recognized Rico, with his corn rolls braided to the back. Shakur always enjoyed the young brother's company. They would have interesting conversations. Rico was from Baltimore but did not talk or act like it, until he's been disrespected. Once a guy was talking crazy to Rico, Rico would ask the guy if he was trying to go somewhere where there weren't any cameras...and that sentence alone deceased the conversation.

"Brother Shakur. Peace," Rico greeted.

"Peace beloved," Shakur returned the greeting.

"All is well?"

"Insha-Allah," Shakur said, meaning if it is the Will of Allah (God), then added "Allahu-ala," meaning Only Allah knows what is best.

Every time Shakur would see young Rico on the rec yard, he would get on Rico's trail, knowing he would have a better conversation. Shakur's intuition told him that Rico would make the perfect protégé.

"Lil bru, what's your hypothesis?"

"To know why you selected me to bring on the teaching in your place?" Rico answered the question with a question. This question had always boiled on Young Rico's brain. He'd been waiting for the opportunity for it to be presented so that he could unfold this burden.

Shakur began to stroke his beard. "It was Allah's doing, little bru. You are one of the chosen ones. You have a position to awaken the people."

Now Rico began to think that Shakur was trying to recruit him, trying to get him to convert and become a Muslim.

"I've claimed no allegiance to no set, cult, or religion. Do you know why?"

"Why, young brother?"

"Because my belief falls in the commonalities of the religions themselves. I look for likenesses, not differences. I believe there is power in the unity of all things. It's just that you have to depict the truth, extract it, and take it for what it is. You have to be conscious, well-learned, and versed. Is it this reason that it's been put forth, your succession of me?"

"Allah has chosen you, little brother," Shakur said, as he smiled and continued to rub his beard. "Please continue to speak on, beloved."

Young Rico's mind refused to allow Shakur to make him a Muslim, but what Rico failed to realize is that Shakur doesn't make people Muslim, Allah makes them Muslim. Shakur saw the desperate look and decided to elaborate more on these subjects, so there would not be miscommunication.

"Lil Rico, you are not self-seeking, you are passionate about the message itself. You have a way of being transparent. The people can see your sincerity! I did not choose you. It is Allah's plan. We are like-minded and kindred in auras. You are about giving the message of awakening. You will go far brother, just believe and keep a pure heart."

"I am tainted, brother, because I hate snitches," Rico said, with the truth being told, that's why he refused to join any type of prison religions.

"There are two types of snitches, Lil Rico, did you know that?" Shakur asked, ready to toy with Young Rico's mind, and thinking to himself that this was a conversation he needed to hear.

"Yes, brother," Rico replied, accepting the challenge and ready to give it to Shakur real and raw. Shakur requested, "Tell me?"

"They are the wet snitch and the dry snitch," Young Rico said, with a serious expression.

"And what separated them?"

"The seven deadly sins."

"Go on," Shakur managed to breathe out, as he warred with himself to hold hostage his laughter.

"The wet snitch is a person who cannot keep any

information to themselves. They have to share all they learn, by the habit of their own nature. They can't help themselves. But they can't hide who they are."

"And the other?" Shakur questioned, continuing to allow Young Rico to lead the conversation.

"The dry snitch is driven by jealousy, envy, greed, lust, etc. They have no self-worth. They will do anything to get ahead. They have no morals or principals. They try to blend in but rarely succeed, because their character precedes them," Rico answered, as he removed his white fitted cap and solid black do-rag.

"Which is more at fault?" Shakur asked.

"I am."

"Why, Lil Rico?"

"Because they both have signs, and I am at fault for not listening. I had the knowledge but did not exercise it. Brother Shakur, it is my fault. Maya Angelou said that if someone shows you who they are, believe them."

"So, I've heard," Shakur replied. No matter what he and Young Rico talked about, he would always allow the youngster to talk in his comfort zone, and he would always end the conversation. "You made a wrong choice, brother. Wake up, focus up, and move forward." Now Shakur's brain really kicked in, and he was 100 percent focused. "I would like to share something with you, beloved. Allah sent three of his angels to destroy a city. They went to the city and did not destroy it, but fled back to Allah and said, Allah, we did not destroy the city, because there was a temple full of knowledgeable monks." Allah replied, "Am I not knowledgeable of all things? When people have knowledge, and do not share it, it goes to waste. The people are dead, walking zombies. Now, Sharp Young Rico, but check this."

"Allah made Adam head of the angels and told them to bow down to Adam. The only angel to question this was Lucifer or Satan. He questioned Allah, and Allah asked him, "Do you know the reason for creation?" Satan said, "I know only what you tell me." Allah then said, "It is for this reason that I place man ahead of you. I need not tell them, but they search."

"Now I'd like to share the story of the million brain. This guy goes into the store. He saw three brains in jars sitting on different shelves. So, he inquiries about the brain on the bottom shelf, Why does that brain cost a quarter million dollars?" The store owner replied, "That was a white guy's brain that died in a motorcycle crash. He lived to be 35 years old, and he made a few million dollars."

"How about the brain in the middle shelf?" the guy questioned.

"The old white man died from old age, natural causes. He lived to reach 89 years old, and he made double-digit millions off of his brain."

The guy pointed to the top shelf, "Why does that brain cost a million dollars?"

"Oh, that's the black man," the store owner revealed, with sadness in his voice.

"He never used it."

"Knowledge unused is knowledge abused," said the guy.

"We're geniuses when it comes to doing negative things," the store owner said. "Yes sir, our young people are masterminds. They need to reverse that energy on doing positive things, and they'll always get a positive result."

Now the guy felt the need to leave the store owner with a jewel of his own.

"You know the difference between a young fool and an old fool?"

"No," the store owner replied immediately. He didn't want to try to answer the question. He did not want to keep the customer holding the answer hostage.

"The old fool was a young fool who refused to change. See, the old fool refused to change out of fear. Now the young fool still has a chance, only if he's brave enough to take on the challenge of change."

# CHAPTER 8

Zeek Bey tried to take a nap during the 4:00 p.m. count, but he couldn't because one of his neighbors talked the whole time. He could hear every word loud and clear through their vent as if he was in the cell with the guys.

"Bruh, you just got to this compound. You haven't been here for five days, and you continue to keep shit stirred up. You got your personal homies going against your other homies!"

"That's their doing," Pecan claimed.

"Naw, bruh, that's YOUR doing. Man, you just left the USP, and you're tryin' to go back!"

"I don't give a fuck."

Pecan's celly continued trying to talk some sense into him. "You been down for how long?"

"Fifteen years."

"And that fifteen years you still haven't learned a damn thing," stated Ally. Pecan's personal homies called him O.G. due to the length of his incarceration, but with truth being told, Pecan was an O.F. (Old Fool). The blind lead the blind.

"Pecan, when do you go home?"

"In six more months, I get the fuck out with no papers."

"You scared to go home?" Ally asked, "You supposed to be tryin' to stay the fuck outta the way, but you get IN the way!"

"What makes you say some dumb shit like that?" Pecan answered the question with a question.

"It speaks for itself," Ally stated, "because you running around here like a fucking chicken with his head cut off. You're stealing people's shit. You're always doing dumb ass shit!"

"I'm doing me!" Pecan said, spreading both arms wide open.

"You doing you," Ally repeated, "You doing shit like you got a death wish."

Pecan started laughing and loudly began to sing 50 Cent's song, "Many men, wish death upon me!"

Zeek Bey was glad when the 4 o'clock count cleared, and the officer unlocked their doors. He walked out of the cell to get away from his neighbor's conversation. Zeek Bey knew Ally was wasting his time and breath with Pecan because Pecan was just stuck on stupid. He stayed doing all the wrong things. Anytime someone was getting into some dumb stuff; you could always count Pecan in. He broke into people's lockers as if he had a license. Pecan's nonsense was only accepted here. He stayed talking tough as if he was a gangster, and the guys actually thought deep down in their hearts that Pecan was a stone, cold killer. Zeek Bey watched the guys downstairs play dominoes until a brother started making his way to the ice machine singing Frosty the Snowman. They were in the month of July. The K-2 had the brother off the chain. He repeated that same line, "Frosty the Snowman!" sixty-six times in a row without stopping. "Frosty the Snowman was a jolly, jolly good man," he'd repeat the sentence once and return to the sixty-six verses. His deep, earthquake voice echoed throughout the unit. The guys that were close to him knew he was high and tripping hard.

"Boy, I need some of THAT!"
"His brain is fried."
"See, that's what that 2 do to you."
"Country boy, please change that tune."
"Give Frosty a hit of that shit!"

They roasted him good and got a good laugh in. The

officer went outside, so he wouldn't have to listen to all that whooping and hollering.

"Frosty got jack!"

"Frosty got SMACK!"

"Frosty high off of K-2, or is it off of crack?" Three of his homies said, making fun of him. The guy paid none of them any mind. He just continued enjoying himself to his so-called "beautiful" song.

"Lord, Lord, Lord," Zeek Bey exhaled, "the people done sent me to the circus." He looked behind him, because of the continuation of the toilet being repeatedly flushed. His other neighbor was washing his clothes in the toilet. Cross would do his sheets and blankets as well. He wouldn't send anything to the laundry. His whites always came back dingy, and his colored clothes would always be dirtier than they were before. But once he finished washing them himself, they will be fresh and clean. The laundry guy washed 1500 inmate's clothes. They stuffed and packed the machines until the clothes don't have much breathing room. Room to race around the cycle freely. Same with the drying machines. Pack, pack, and stuff, stuff. The clothes didn't come back thoroughly dry. They would mildew. Zeek Bey's neighbor was a neat freak. He always kept the cleanest cell in the unit. All his clothes were ironed and neatly hanging on his rack. The toilet did wonders for the guy.

"Ten-minute move."

"Ten-minute move."

"To early pill line."

"To the rec yard." The intercom announced.

"If you guys are going out on this 10-minute move, let's go now," the unit officer announced.

"You go," someone shouted to the officer, "Fuck that move, and fuck YOU!"

The officer had better sense than to respond to that

nonsense. Why entertain that negativity? Besides, what could he say to a man that had eight hundred and seventy-two years, or to someone with a life sentence? The officer had to do the wise thing, and that was to allow that propaganda or unprofessional conduct to go in one ear and out of the other one. Nine times out of ten, the guy who made that crazy statement was going to beg up every word. These guys were doing 85 percent of their time; they were fearless, they didn't fear death. They would welcome it. NWA's words were ingrained on their tongues: "Fuck the Police."

The COs were smart enough to sucker duck as well. They weren't trying to do what the dummies do, by going head-on with Billy Badass. Smart COs always acted as if they didn't hear the crazy language. They had nothing to win and weren't about to put their lives on the line. The devil would have to find a no-brain to fulfill them shoes. The ones that God guides, no one can misguide.

Zeek Bey and the dominoes crew headed to the rec yard. He saw here and now the opportunity to talk with them because Zeek Bey also enjoyed the game. Besides, this was how most guys did their time and killed the clock.

"Big Guy, you must be a great dominoes player," Zeek Bey addressed Peewee, who was the smallest among them.

"I'm far from a square," Peewee replied.

"I always hear a guy say, don't let Peewee win," Zeek Bey said, smiling.

"Yeah, he says that every time he sees me playing," Peewee confessed.

"He also says, if you wanna win, play Peewee," Big reminded him.

"Big, you the great bum," Peewee said, retaliating.

"Yeah, that's me," Big confirmed.

"Y'all be playin' partners?" Zeek Bey asked, "Teams?"

"Naw, every man for himself," Rock answered.

Once they reached the rec yard gate, the young white man officer's loud mouth was the only voice being heard, because when he showed up, he showed out.

"Inmates, y'all know y'all have to pay taxes because we need them raggedy ass stamps so that we can pay our snitches!" Once he made that statement, he'd always be calling guys to the side to pat search them, hoping to find over 60 stamps in their possession so that he could confiscate them. While he was getting him some practice by shaking down this guy that did not have a pot to piss in nor a window to throw it out of, the guy said, "I love this shit. You need to put somethin' IN one of my pockets, cause I'm the lowest, the poorest, and most definitely need it the most."

"I do love this shit," the officer replied, by saying one of the names that they have given him.

Another guy was heading towards the officer. He was riding dirty and couldn't stand a shakedown, so he said loud and clear, "I ain't got nothin' but a hard dick and bubblegum, and I'm fresh out of bubblegum."

"You call it D, but once it turns dark, you become all coochie, coochie, wal-lie," the officer said, laughing. "You musta forgot, I used to work your unit, and at night your whole unit would be hollering, look at Sha-na-na with them Daisy Dukes on!"

The guy had to laugh along with that because he didn't know how to respond to that one. Everyone who heard that ran with it and told other guys the joke the crazy officer said today. The officer signaled for another guy to step to the side so that he could pat search him. "You know why I pulled you over, right?"

"No, why?" The guy answered the question with a question.

"Because you ain't killed yourself!" The officer said. He

joked with the whole compound, everybody and all day. Guys would scream across the compound to the officer, and his second name became Kill Yaself.

Zeek Bey broke away from the dominoes crew, making his way to the law library. A brother ahead of him said to his homie, “Man, I'm hungry enough to eat a bare ass. Baby, them crackers got butter from the duck. Bruh, they worked the dog shit out of me today in Unicor. I can't lie, they got their money's worth today, if they don't get it tomorrow.”

Coming to prison is like being placed in a rocket and being sent to the moon because everything our forefathers fought for doesn't apply, because rules and regulations are a world of difference. Prison is a reinstatement of slavery, the point being a whole month's wages can be from $5 to $50 for working 5-days a week, 8-hours a day. Commissary prices are 3 or 4 times higher than street stores' prices. Unicor is a multibillion-dollar business performed mostly by people with restitution payments to make. The sweatshop's hard day of labor equaled to anywhere from a few nickels to a few quarters a day, but to some guys, it's their heaven. Their only means of survival and on the other hand, it's also a blessing to some other guys, because they're stacking and packing, so they'll have a few dollars when the gates opens.

Zeek Bey finally walked through the law library doors. He immediately spotted Wendall “Buck” Jefferson, and Rivera Marshall huddled around the second table. He stood a few feet away, giving them their privacy out of respect. Zeek Bey waited patiently until Buck recognized his presence.

Zeek Bey always saw Young Rivera and Buck together. He knew they were homies, as well as Buck was assisting Rivera to win back his freedom.

“I'm almost finished with completing this motion for Bo-

Deen," Buck said, letting Rivera know to hold his train of thought because Buck did not need to lose his train of thought.

Once he finished with the homie's papers, Buck stood and stretched. "I need to play a game or two of basketball," he said.

"Naw, you don't need to," Rivera stated, "You might mess around and hurt that ankle again."

You know it ain't healed good yet." Truthfully, Rivera was trying to put some insurance on getting Buck to file his petition. The sooner, the better.

"You right," Buck replied.

"In another week you should be good," Rivera said, smiling.

Buck noticed Zeek Bey faking, as though the library novels interested him. "Zeek Bey, what's up, bruh?"

Zeek Bey placed the novel back on the shelf, not caring if he placed the book back into its rightful place or not. He didn't want to delay any further his conversation with Buck. Shakur told him about Buck knowing what he knew concerning the law, and that Buck would be the best candidate to assist, because he was going to keep it 100 with him and not try to beat him out of the cookies and candy as the other jailhouse lawyers did. Buck wasn't just after the papers; he was going to take pride in his work and going to do his petition as if he were working towards his own freedom.

"Zeek, you heard from Brother Shakur?" Buck asked. "They're on lockdown," Zeek Bey replied.

"Another stabbing or killing," Buck predicted.

"Black and Hispanic riot," Zeek Bey updated.

"I hope Brother Shakur's alright," Buck said, out of love and concern. Him and Shakur carried it like family, two brothers from different mothers.

"Shakur has the same protector that Moses had protecting

him against the pharaoh," Zeek Bey publicized.

Buck was wise enough to know that Zeek Bey was stating that Allah was Shakur's protector, because he, himself, had heard Shakur admit that Allah was his everything and his provider as well. Shakur would not hesitate to confess that he could not do anything without Allah. And if there was no Allah, there would be no him.

Shakur had no shame when it comes to his God. He always spoke highly of Allah. Shakur would mention Allah in any and every conversation.

"A'oothu billahi min ash-shaytaa nir-rajeem," (I seek refuge in Allah from Satan the Outcast.)

"A'hamdu lillaah," (All praises and thanks are to Allah.)

"Yarhamullallaah," (May Allah have mercy upon you.)

"Astaghfirullasha wa'atoobu ilayhi," (I seek the forgiveness of Allah and repent to him.)

"Subhaana Rabbiyal-a'laa," (Glory is to my Lord, the most high.)

"Ghufraanaka," (I seek your forgiveness.)

"Bismillaah," (In the name of Allah.)

"Laa'ilaaha 'illallaah, allaahu 'akbar," (There is none worthy of worship but Allah, Allah is the Greatest.)

Buck got back to the situation at hand. "Zeek Bey, I finished your petition. I want you to send it out tomorrow, send it certified."

"I can do that," Zeek Bey said, excited.

"Brother Zeek, this should make you a free man." "Insha-Allah."

"Yeah, if it's God's will," Buck said the Arabic language in English.

"I made an extra copy for you to keep," Buck said, while pulling the papers from his folder.

"Buck, I appreciate it."

"Brother Zeek, I wish I could free everybody. Especially

myself!"
"Allahu ala."

Buck did not know that word's meaning, so he asked, because the only dumb questions were the ones you didn't ask.

"What does Allahu-ala mean?"
"Only Allah knows what's best."
"Shakur always says Allah is the best of planners."
"He's right."

ONE WITHOUT A DREAM AND WITHOUT A VISION WILL SURELY PERISH.

# CHAPTER 9

John Lockett, Spunk, Pud, and Itchy sat on the bench watching the softball game. These two A-league teams showed up and showed out. They were in the last inning. Outfield was ahead by three runs. Valentine walked up to bat; he had three men on bases. So, with the bases loaded, he planned to tie the score up and take this game into overtime, if not win the game. Valentine was known for getting a couple of home runs per game. He had two under his belt for today, and now he was determined to get the third one. This was definitely a need and not a want.

Cornbread stood on the pitcher's mound feeling no different than Valentine. This game was definitely a need for him and his team, and not a want. If Cornbread could pull this game off, they would make the playoffs.

"Let's go, Bread!" Lockett cheered Cornbread on. "We need this game!"

"I got Valentine, youngster," Cornbread stated. He actually won the best pitcher of the year, three years in a row. No one could out-pitch the sixty-eight-year-old man.

"Let's go, old man," Valentine challenged Cornbread, "Come on so I can knock this ball over the fence as I have done twice earlier in the game."

"That's old news, youngster," Cornbread replied, smiling. "I'ma be the new news."

"I can't do nothing if you keep on holding the ball! Don't get scared now," Valentine said.

"I'ma get my super curveball ready," Cornbread let the cat out of the bag, "Youngster, y'all ain't ready for my curveball!"

"Bread, you holding up the game with all that

talking!" Nard joked. "This is y'all's last inning, both of y'all are finna be on the sideline! Then y'all can do all the talking and dancing that y'all wanna do."

"Valentine, here it comes," Cornbread said, as he put both hands behind his back. "Valentine, you either go hard or go home."

As Cornbread was releasing his speech, he was also releasing the ball. Valentine drew the bat and swung with all his might. The bat connected with a little under half of the ball, causing the softball to speed backward instead of forward. The ball landed over the fence behind Valentine.

"Strike one!" the umpire announced.

"Chino, you said you were going to knock the ball over the fence!" Valentine's celly joked. "You knocked it over the fence forward twice, so now you wanted to get you one backward too, during the game."

Valentine didn't reply. He wanted to stay focused on the pitcher. "Old man, give me your best shot. Is that all you've got?"

"O'le hell, you couldn't handle THAT one!" Cornbread confirmed. "I'ma do it again youngster, just keep on closing your eyes and swing as hard as you can!"

The white, dusty softball danced through the air once again. Valentine knew this here was the one, the home run that he needed.

He swung with all his might. As soon as the bat connected, the ball did another ballet dance and immediately went spinning and speeding to the left, out of bounds. Valentine wanted it to be considered a foul ball, but since he had one strike against him already, the ball was legally called.

"Strike!" the umpire shouted.

Tanger Eye held two fingers into the air and shouted,

"Bread, two down and one mo' to go! We need this one, bread!"

"Strike two!" the umpire publicized, giving the rec crowd the count.

"Cornbread, man, you're licking your thumb and putting spit on the ball!" someone joked.

"Sssshhh," Cornbread breathed out and said, "See no evil, hear no evil, speak no evil," and he released the ball.

Valentine swung and made a solid connection. The ball went flying full speed ahead towards the pitcher. Cornbread acted from experience and not out of fear. He ran getting out of the ball's way, and once the ball reached within arm's length, threw his right arm behind his back, catching the ball. Valentine didn't have time to witness the backward catch, because he was too busy trying to get a base hit, so one, if not two of his teammates, could make it to home plate, giving them a score or two along with another batter up. Cornbread timed Valentine perfectly. Valentine's feet were in the air getting ready to stomp first base, but the ball beat him by a hair. The first baseman caught the ball and touched Valentine with it, putting him out twice.

"Valentine, I got you out twice with the same hit," Cornbread said, bragging. "How'd that manage to happen?"

"They say if you keep living, you'll see all types of things, old man," Valentine said, with good spirits.

"It took me 68 years to do that," Cornbread said.

"Bread baby, you sho nuff gonna be hell when you get 69," Tanger Eye predicted.

The rec officer over sports took Cornbread's picture and added him to the hall of fame. Inmates would see the photo mounted on the wall and recapture the event, when the old head had single-handedly outshined Valentine.

Playa congratulated Cornbread on the victory as well as the entire compound, because he was their old head here. The white old man would play full-court basketball with the young black guys. Everyone respected and had much love for Cornbread.

Killer waited patiently until Playa walked off from the crowd.

"Texas, Texas, Texas," Killer said, once he captured Playa's attention. He walked over and started talking.

"Texas, what's up? I haven't seen you in a minute," Killer said.

Since Tray's killing, Playa had stayed his distance. Once he got off of work, he'd go to the rec yard and work out, watch Cornbread work the horseshoes, or play basketball. He'd be at the opposite places that Killer would be; besides, they didn't have anything in common. Chase was his partner.

"Woady, I miss Round," Playa said. He always addressed killer with 'Woady' and Chase by 'Round.'

"Yeah, I miss my Round too, ya heard me?" said Killer.

"Woady, you know that inmate.com is a mother," Playa warned, alerting Killer that his name was coming out of other people's mouths constantly.

"These niggas holler 'bout they gangsta," Killer said. "These niggas do more gossipin' than females. All they do is sit around and watch shit, wait on shit to happen, so they can talk about it or go and tell."

"They're walking cameras, Woady," Playa stated. "Sometimes I call 'em rubbernecks."

"I thought they say that people in the U.S.P don't snitch?" asked Killer.

"Woady, you got snitches everywhere," Playa said, being honest. "And like you said, the key word is 'they

SAY.'"

"Shit," Killer mumbled, rubbing his head, "I need a drink. Where can I get me something to drink from?"

"I haven't had a drink since I drunk with you and Round. I don't drink from people I don't deal with on a daily basis. I have to know the person or have to watch him before I drink his liquor. Woady, everybody who makes liquor ain't clean," Playa said.

After conversing with Playa, Killer needed some liquor. He dapped Playa and told him he'd holler back the next time they crossed paths in traffic. There were 1600 people on the pound, and Killer knew someone would be able to point him into the direction that he needed to go. Once Killer got that alcohol in his system, he could focus better... at least, that was the delusion he would often feed to himself.

"Damn, I need my medication," he whispered, talking about the jailhouse wine or liquor.

Anything with some alcohol. Killer walked around the rec yard as a predator looking for his prey, and it did not take long before he stumbled upon the herd of softball players. Immediately after the game, they'd huddle around third base and pull out the ten-gallon batch that had been brewing for a good two weeks. They didn't have anything to strain the wine with, so they used Tank's socks. They did know the old fool's feet, and shoes kept his cell stinking, nor about his Athlete's Foot. They just needed the wine strained, and the (OF) overheard their conversation and went into the bathroom, removing his socks. A minute later, Tank was screaming, "I got a pair of socks for two stamps!" Everyone knew Tank sold things for no more than two stamps. He would two-stamp the compound to death. The wine was in a keg; the guys were filling their soda cans, so the rec officers would think they were celebrating with sodas as usual. The wine had plenty of alcohol in it, but the dirty taste overruled the alcohol. Most guys poured their wine back into the keg. The alcoholics though, "More for me!"

Killer worked his way amongst the crowd, "Hey, my friend. I'm trying to buy some shine or wine. Can you help me?"

Mr. Friendly passed Killer the soda can he'd previously drank out of. "Taste this and see if you like it," he said. Mr. Friendly was trying to make a sale; he wasn't going to inform Killer that the liquor tasted like dirt, because what's good for the goose isn't good for the gander.

Killer drank half the can and paused, sucking on his tongue. "What you think?" Mr. Friendly asked. Killer showed him what he thought by turning the can up to his mouth for seconds. Once the can was drained, Killer sucked on the top, not wanting to waste a drop of the wine.

"It's alright," Killer claimed, "How much for two gallons?"

"You make me an offer," Mr. Friendly said, not wanting to cause bad blood, and keeping accountable that he'd have to look into Killer's face every day, as well as hoping to keep Killer as a regular customer.

"Fifteen dollars a gallon," Killer stated, going five dollars under the normal rate.

"I'll do you better than that," Mr. Friendly said, "Just give me five books." He knocked five dollars off of the thirty dollars.

Killer did not rest until he drank all the wine. All five of his senses started to go crazy. He saw and heard things that no one else was able to see or hear. His body began to rain with sweat. As he felt dizzy, his tongue became super heavy, and Killer began throwing up to the point that it began to choke him. He vomited so much blood until he passed out, the guys had no choice but to notify the officer that Killer desperately needed assistance, and they really did mean right now. "CO! CO! CO! Man down!! CO!"

---

If a person could make it through the difficult tasks in USP Petty Rock, surely he could also go deep sea diving and swim through a billion shark eaters with a bloody finger and live to tell about it. Here, the staff members are gorillas. Gangstas and natural born killers have the right away and the heart to be as ruthless as they want to be. These individual characters changed momentarily - yes, they had split personalities.

Lt. Keli was a chubby guy, who would always be getting his lunch money taken and getting slapped around in school. His bullying began from the very first day of school, until his last day of school. Correct, he got pushed over for 18 years. Now he's here to show that he's the top dog, and claiming he put the letter 'b' in the word bully. He ruled with an iron fist, not with sense. His eyes sunk back into the sockets. Keli's fat jaws stuck out like his mouth was stuffed with cotton. His wrinkled forehead made his coward tail give off the image of a tough person, but his squeaky voice gave him away every time.

Lt. Keli already knew that asking questions is only the policy of the BOP, and besides, that's only one of the policies that he'd abide by. Bright and early there'd be snitches posted by his office, ready and willing to spill their guts, updating him on the prohibited activities, promising to put faces to every event before leaving that office, by pointing out every Tom, Dick, and Harry from the desktop computer. The group of snitches snitched to have a safety net: snitch to get transferred, snitch just to stay in his good graces, snitch out of jealousy.

Lt. Keli had the officers to secure the area Killer

passed out on, so the so-called prison ambulance could drive the golf cart into the rec yard and lay the bed board beside him, properly secure him, and take him to the institution infirmary.

"Before the day is out, you have my word, I'm going to find out which one of you sold this dying inmate some dope," Lt. Keli said, to no one in particular.

"That man ain't had no dope, man," someone said.

Lt. pointed to another inmate that he thought he knew was selling drugs. "You're the number one biggest drug dealer on the compound."

"I can't stop you from guessing, but I can keep you from knowing," the guy said smiling, "Lt., around here, you have to believe half of what you see and none of what you heard."

"Trust me, I know y'all who be selling that dope," Lt. Keli said.

"Lt., man, I ain't had no helicopter, no airplane, no submarines. They gave me 65 years. And I was just the smoker." The guy said, knowing that everyone wanted to be the kingpin, but no one yearns to be the smoker.

"Lt., you know who got that dope, playboy?" another guy asked, joking with the Lt.

"Who! Who! Who got it?" Lt. Keli asked, out of anger and being hostile.

"These nuts!"

---

Shakur and Sten X lived in the state of being Hasan; they were absolutely sincere to Allah in one's self. They worshiped Allah as though they saw him, knowing that although they do not see Allah, Allah sees them. They trusted in Allah whole-heartedly and believed in Allah's angels, books, and messengers, the last day, the garden and the fire, and everything is by the decree of Allah, both good and evil. These brothers remember Allah constantly. Avoid what is forbidden, keep within limits prescribed by Allah. Shakur followed Sunnah of Prophet Muhammad (May Allah bless him and grant him peace). Shakur and Sten X could recite the Qur'an. That's how they were able to gain more knowledge and wisdom. They pledged their loyalty to Allah, and Allah alone. Like some people work their entire lives, Shakur and Sten X were working to get to what Muslims called Paradise (the hereafter). In the Qur'an Surah 2, Ayat 208 said: "O you who believe! Enter perfectly into Islam, by obeying all the rules and regulations of the religion of Islam and follow not in the footsteps of Satan (the Devil). Verily, he is to you a plain enemy." They always spent a great deal of time repenting to Allah for their past and future sins. Neither do they seek the good of this world, always asking Allah not to leave them alone, not even for a blink of an eye.

They adhered accordingly only to what Allah has prescribed for them, and only Allah can remove one's shortcomings and illness. A human process because humans strive. Wrongdoings will occur through the hands of Muslims. Sometimes people will make the ridiculous misconceptions of terrorists, as well as corrupted Muslims that stray away from their rightful deed. These favor tricks and submissions to their desire with the truth and falsehood. Don't become selfish, for Allah's sake don't waste effort, nor stray away from the body of the righteous Muslims. Stay on your deen, do only the appropriate things that Allah has prescribed for you and your religion. Don't allow anything or anyone to put you back into the state of mental blandness (In Islam it's known as Jahaliya), not to fall back into ignorance after one has the rightful duties. One must be the best example of mankind. One can bring people into the fold of Islam or can run people away from Islam. Allah only favors the ones or one, who is righteously on their deen, doing the work only of Allah. They are truly Allah's servants. After every difficulty, there will come ease. Everything has to be done according to the Qur'an and Sunnah; there is no other way. Shakur wants for his brothers what he wants for himself. He wanted all the Muslims to go to paradise. He also wanted all the good things Allah can give them as a whole because Allah says "All the good is from him, and all the evil is from oneself and Satan, the devil."

Allah says every man wears his own sin. For every good deed, he'll be rewarded ten or more. For every act of evil that individual will get one sin against him. So, every act of evil is a sin and can only be righted by repenting. Dragging your brother into the hellfire is caused by inviting him to fitnah, which means forbidden things in the Islamic rules. Enjoy the good and forbid the evil. Another way to drag your brother into the hellfire is when you see him doing harmful acts, and you don't try to stop it. You definitely wear that sin. If you can't stop it with your hands, then speak out against it, and if that doesn't work, then hate it in your heart. When a Muslim hates the wrongdoing in their heart, it's like a small prayer to Allah.

Shakur and Sten X finally noticed all the commotion towards the gate, as well as heard someone say that dude fell out from drinking wine, and now the youngster was on the gate clowning around with the L.T.

"Keli on foolishness," Shakur stated.

"So is the youngster," Sten X reminded him.

"You think we can drill a hole into the youngster's head, pour in the knowledge, and seal it back up?" Shakur asked, in a serious tone.

"It would be nice," Sten X replied.

"I'm tired of watching the news and 48-hours because the younger generations just TRYING to tear the door down to come to jail or be killed. When are they going to wake up?" Shakur said with emotion.

“They're not going to like it here,” Sten X stated, slowly wheeling himself back and forth. “This place is worse than the streets. All we can do is travel around in circles all day and every day.”

“Allah has given every male and female a purpose,” Shakur stated, “As well as a gift.”

“Wake up, my young generation,” Sten X said.

“We just have to continue to guide them with sincere advice,” Shakur promised.

“They're learning the hard way that Satan is here to destroy them and rob them of all the beautiful blessings that Allah has for them,” Sten X reminded him.

“Allahu-ala,” Shakur said.

“You're right, Shakur,” Sten X agreed, “Only Allah knows what's best.”

Force... Optimism ... Communication ... Unity ... Sacrifice ... Understand ... Persevere

# CHAPTER 10

Things in life happen for reasons and by season. It was written by the will of Allah that life's challenging circumstances would take place on a such-and-such date, to such-and-such. Most people allow the cruelty of the world to be their teaching, and with this misconception, eventually, a young male will encounter multiple struggles.

Little did Chase know, he'd visit a numerous variety of holdovers before his trial begins. They would keep transferring him before he got too comfortable. Only Allah knows how many nights Chase will sleep under a roof before the guard comes to his cell door and tells him to get ready to be transferred in twenty minutes. Sometimes you might be in the building for only a couple of hours, and they'll inform you that it's time to get ready to roll out. Now if you've been a problem, and they have you on what's called a "diesel ride," you'll stay on a bus or plane, and you'll stay moving. Your mail will never catch you; you'll never get a good night's rest. Your butt and back promise to constantly ache. You'll never eat a hot meal, just cold cuts, and peanut-butter-and-jelly sandwiches. The system will ride you as the wild horse you proclaim to be, and you are guaranteed to go sight-seeing for six months to a good year.

One hour of Rec five days a week, each male assigned to their individual cage. Here's the only time they'll get the opportunity to communicate with one another. When the Rec Officer comes by their cell door, he'll holler, "REC?", And here's when each individual gets the chance to make the beautiful request to be placed in the cage beside the person of their choice, so they talk for the hour or exercise together. But for some strange reason, Chase always got placed in the cage next to the brother called Knowledge, and Knowledge was a very much approachable brother. It never failed that he would bring books outside with him. While the others exercised, conversed, or just enjoyed the sunshine or fresh air, Knowledge would be studying the world, 24/7, constantly trying to break down and digest the Creator's powerful words.

Last week, a guard asked Knowledge why he carried the books out to Rec. Knowledge replied,

"To study."

"You're locked down 23 hours straight, 24 hours straight on Saturday and Sunday. So, what do you do then?"

"Study."

"Study," the officer frowned and repeated. "It ain't that much studying in the world."

"CO, I been into everything but a casket. Now I have learned that God is a merciful God, and loves when we repent. As well as I have learned that everyone has a purpose in life, they must uncover."

"So, since you claim I don't comprehend so well, then tell me my purpose in life."

"Only Allah knows what's best, but since you're an asshole, and always out to go to the extreme to make our days harder and more miserable, I would say your purpose in life is to test the believers. To see if we can stand strong on the Lord's word. Remember, even Jesus was tested."

The officer would do every little thing he could do to the inmates. Some days he'd tiptoe down the ranges and wouldn't make his presence known, so there'd be fewer people for him to take to Rec. The white officer was racist, and some days he couldn't hide it. He often lied about it raining outside or stated it was colder outside during the winter. He'd roll the shower to their door while they slept and said they refused, the same thing he would say about their Rec. He would misuse and abuse his authority because, in his mind, he actually thought he was the chief.

"So, you think God can protect you from me?"

"That's not a question, that's the truth."

"Then that we'll see."

"I believe in God, not man-made law. God has the final say-so."

Officer Cearse stopped in front of cell door 203. "Man, you say you were a soldier on the front line? You were a coward on the front line."

Officer Big Sake said, "I used to work with Special Ed kids." The two officers entertained Cell 203.

"Man, y'all get the fuck off of the range with that bullshit, leave the man the fuck alone! It's too damn early for that bullshit!" shouted Cell 201, at 5:01 a.m., breakfast time.

"Man, I'm tired of fucking up and doing dumb shit. I do stupid shit just to be doing something. I'm in the fucking Hole; I can't call my kids... boy, these crackers broke me. I'm through with the bullshit. They ain't got no problems with riding 'ya and most definitely got a place to hide ya. I'm finna change, I'ma do a whole 360, I'm gonna transform into a good nigga," 200 said, through the cell door.

Now Officer Big Sake stated he worked with Special Ed kids for a variety of reasons. He called some guys 'special' due to their character. One guy had the misconception that he had all the answers. He refused to admit that he didn't know something. He was going to produce some type of answers. He was doing the right thing by trying to better himself by programming, so he'd go out better than he came in. But he's unstable; his knowledge comes from the books he read and not from experience. He doesn't have the common sense and often became the butt end of someone's joke, as well as made a straight up-and-down donkey out of himself.

He was always asking Officer Big Sake what type of kids he'd worked with, and little did he know that he was one of the kids that the officer called special. Whoever Officer Big Sake told his favorite line to; he'd call that individual special.

Another guy served twenty years, stayed out for six months, came back with a fresh twenty-five years. And keep in mind, 85 percent of that sentence had to be served. Old boy stayed bitter and miserable. He stayed doing all the wrong things, which is called chasing death. He stayed having problems with cellies, can't get along with anyone, always fighting, and the crazy part was he'd never win nor did he know how to fight. He alone needed a friend, needed a hug by him not knowing how to approach people. He did everything in a butthole way… and that's how he was able to have a conversation with the people. And to him, that's how he called "having a good report" with the individual or individuals. Now he'd have the right away to ask you if you're doing alright daily, and escalate to numerous other off-the-wall conversations. These guys were seeking attention. He too loved to see Officer Big Sake. He'd grin from ear-to-ear when he's being told, concerning the Special Ed kids in the Malcolm X movie. Malcolm X was going up the stairs, and a guy raced to the bottom of the steps and was hollering crazy stuff to Malcolm X, saying, "He wasn't nothing," etc. Malcolm X stopped in his tracks and faced the guy. Malcolm explained to his people, "The guy doesn't mean any harm," and then said loud and clear, "Get the brother a suit and some shoes."

The guy hollered "For real!?" He just needed to be

accepted and feel accepted. Once these individuals get the required attention, they'll calm down. Officer Big Sake became their daddy, big brother, as well as their expensive babysitter. Every time one tried to be a high style to the big guy; he'd prove to them he's a giant within the heart. Officer Big Sake finessed the game, he'd think over the situation instead of fighting the situation. One youngster calls him every disrespectful name that could or would be produced, talked about his mother, wife, and family. They weren't smart enough to get him off of his square. He pacified, baby-bottled, and spoon-fed the prisoners. He did everything with common sense, and no, it doesn't take a scientist to teach a wise one.

---

Big Ro's upper body was soaking wet with sweat. He felt as though someone had poured a whole gallon of water on him. The dream had his heart rate beating with the march of a marching band. His blood pressure was through the roof. Both pillows, his sheets, and blankets were on the floor. Sten was running backward when he exchanged gunfire with the second detective.

"POW!"

"POW!"

"POW!"

"POW!"

Big Ro could still hear as if the event had unfolded behind his eyelids. "Sten! No, Sten!" he mumbled, as the tears moonwalked down his face. Sten's pants began to dance down his waist with every step he took backward. "No Sten. Oh, God, no." Big Ro cried out. Sten made a mistake, and the detective took full advantage of the opportunity, knowing he'd go hard or he wasn't going home. It would be him or Sten. The Detective exercised his finger, and he watched with pride as the bullets penetrated Sten's body.

As Sten's back connected with the concrete, the Detective continued to use his body as target practice. He didn't feel the need to take one bullet back home with him, especially not tonight. Sten had killed his partner, so he saw it as an eye for an eye and a tooth for a tooth. He took matters into his own hands that night. He was the judge, the jury, and the executioner. Once he reached Sten's body, he was still squeezing the trigger until he was completely out of bullets.

The sound of his empty gun was only gas to a fire; it only infuriated him. The Detective kicked the gun out of Sten's grip and picked up the other pistol Sten managed to drop while reaching for his pants. The Detective kneeled down beside Sten's head, and with anger on his face, he greeted, "You're a dead nigga."

Big Ro hollered like a mother weeping for her only baby, "NO, please don't kill my son."

"POW."

Big Ro's eyes blanked. He did not want to let go of the dream. "No, Sten. Sten, I'm sorry!" Big Ro cupped both hands over his eyes. He saw himself also kneeled beside Sten, looking into the Detective's eyes. And in Big Ro's mind, he wanted to give the Detective the very same medication he'd given to Sten. The only thing that interfered with the program was the Detective's backup.

The blue and red police lights behind Big Ro's eyelids caused him to immediately abandon the dream against his will. He sat up in bed, the wetness of his body forcing him to feel his chest as if he too had taken a couple of rounds. "Damn, Sten! You should have got him too. Your big ass pants were your downfall. Son, why couldn't you wear your own damn size!? Sten, I'm sorry! It was my fault... it was all my fault."

There is a certain hesitation about dwelling on events of the past. On the one hand, it creates an atmosphere of determinism, which removes the volitional possibilities of people to alter their condition. It tends to excuse the perpetuation of past events, which could be altered, simply by initiative. It preoccupies people unnecessarily and purposelessly with old hurts, tending old wounds. It is an emotional tirade that ultimately provides no constructive solutions for the present. Those who deny the lessons of the past, are doomed to repeat them. Those who fail to recognize that the past is a shaper of the present, and the hand of yesterday, continuing to write on the slate of today, leave themselves vulnerable by not realizing the impact of influences, which do serve to shape their lives.

# CHAPTER 11

Zeek Bey danced around as he looked into the mirror. When Michael Jackson's song, *Man in the Mirror*, came on, he'd been sho-nuff cutting up, dancing as if he were the King of Pop. The lyrics began to register, and his brain went into overdrive. *"I'm talking to the man in the mirror; I'm asking him to change his ways. We want the world to be a better place; we have to make that change."*

Zeek Bey wiped the sweat from his face. "Mike, that is so true, thank you." Zeek Bey had heard the right words at the right time. "When I was young, I was fast to react and slow to think. Now I'm more of a thinker and slow on acting, because some of us are not able to see the bigger picture," he said out loud.

There was no one in his cell with him. Sometimes Zeek Bey felt the need to drop jewels with his mouth and hear them with his own two ears. This was what he called talking to himself, without talking back, avoiding the saying, *It's okay to talk to yourself, but just don't answer back.*

"The people blindly following their misguided leaders. They need to join my mission by being sincerely obedient to Allah, and if you count the blessings of Allah, you'll learn, the blessings will never be able to be counted."

Zeek Bey's little one-on-one privacy was invaded by the CO, announcing he was about to begin his morning census count. The officer needed to know the correct number and names of the inmates in the Unit.

"I love my job, because I can do whatever the fuck I

want to do," the officer said loud, proud, and clear so everyone could know he was their babysitter for eight hours. "Don't nobody move, but the ones I know is orderliness, and I don't know no fucking body," he continued, shouting.

"I love this shit!" someone screamed, which they'd nicknamed the officer. "Honestly, to God, I do," the officer confirmed.

"Go kill ya-self," someone else hollered, the officer's other nickname.

"Sir, sir, please, do complete that mission after I finish my census count," the officer joked back at him.

"Bru, as soon as crazy-man finishes his census count, I'm going outside to get outta his way. This fool done showed up, and he's gonna show out," Salad said.

"I heard that, I heard that," the CO said, "Now go and kill ya-self."

"Brothers, don't let your life get away. Opportunity, blessing, and prayer changes things. Ask God to give you strength to assist you with the corrections of your situation. Prayer is the whole wide world tool of weapon," Zeek Bey mumbled.

As soon as the ten-minute-move was announced, a majority of the guys in Zeek Bey's Unit immediately went to Rec to escape the Unit officer.

Zeek Bey sat close to the chess table. He enjoyed watching Player and T.T., from Florida, play. They had a serious grudge match. They did not play anyone else. Always these two. Outside, Zeek Bey always heard plenty of jargons, meaning unintelligent talk.

A group of youngsters sat on top of the tables, knowing that the rec man was going to have a baby about them, sitting on the table. They figured he'd get tired of telling them to get down before they got tired of sitting on it.

"Man, you holler at the teacher, so you can get in the welding class? Boy, I'm gonna get this trade, so I can secure my future," stated Gump.

"Bruh, that cracker's playing games," Markei replied, "He told me to come back in two weeks, cause he has a full roster. He needs to see if anybody dropped out. I'm not gonna kiss that cracker's ass. Fuck him, and fuck that class!"

"That's right, Markei," Jit instigated, "Fuck that cracker!"

"Markei, but you'll kiss a nigga's ass that you don't like for that funky ass K-2 and spit- a- rettes. The shit that the white man has to offer, it can take you a long way. Give your dumb ass a career," Gump reminded.

"He's right, Markei," said Jay.

"Bru, Gump did say a mouthful then," Jit agreed.

"Damn nigga, who's side you on?" Markei looked in Jit's direction. "One minute you on a nigga's team, then you jump ship and ride with fat boy Gump!"

"I'm with you, but Gump's right this time," Jit smoothed out.

"Man, I'ma holla back at the school teacher in two weeks like he said," Markei announced, but truly, he was talking to Gump.

"Gump, man, Markei just don't want to miss out on The Young and the Restless," Jay said, just talking junk.

"You'll be right beside me when The Young and the Restless is on, too," Markei replied to Jay.

"Boy, stop," Jit said, "I can't wait to see what happens tomorrow."

"You should've been in front of that TV instead of in the streets," Gump said.

The rec officer came around and put their clowning to an end by telling them to get off of the rec table, and that they needed to sit down on the table in the proper form like everyone else.

"What makes y'all special?" the Rec Officer asked, with both arms spread wide open, "What makes y'all group of guys so different?" he requested.

"We are different," Jit said. He and the rec man stayed into it concerning that table.

"Very different," Markei spoke, taking sides with Jit.

"We make a great big difference," Jay said, and truly did not really know what he'd just stated.

"Y'all heard what I said. The next time I catch one of y'all on top of my table, I'm going to lock that ass up," the Rec man popped slick, as usual.

"Man, the Hole don't scare nobody," Jay replied.

"Yeah, yeah, it ain't nothing but another part of the jail," Jit stated.

"It ain't gonna stop nobody's time, a nigga's time is still gonna go on," Markei added his two cents.

The rec man stopped and turned back towards them, "Who wants to go to the Hole first? I'll have all of y'all put in the SHU."

"Man, y'all leave the man alone," Gump encouraged, "So he can get the fuck on."

"Yeah man, go on," Jay waved the rec man off. "Go back to ya business so we can get back to our business, my nigga."

The rec man hated it with a passion, when the brothers would be talking to him, as if he was a brother as well. He'd turn red in the face, and so would his neck. The rec man wasted no time escaping away from their presence. A nigga is not a colored person, but an ignorant person. Any Race can be a nigga, according to one's action and characteristics.

"Yeah, we'll holla at'cha, playa," Gump said.

Zeek Bey saw Gump as their leader, and thought this would be a beautiful opportunity as ever, to get in where fits in. Yes, to be a polka dot and find his spots. He addressed the group.

"Peace and love, young brothers, I'm with the Moorish Science Temple. We're having a beautiful service Friday night at 6 p.m. It will be a great honor if you can come."

"I'm not putting no invisible leash around my neck and putting the leash in no one's hand," Jit fired off.

"I believe in God, I believe there's a higher power, but I don't do the religion thing," Jay said to him.

"I got too much other bullshit to do," Markei said, smiling. "I'm just being honest."

"Bruh, I'm a trend setter, I'm not a follower," Gump replied, "My blood type is rare. You won't find too many more guys like me."

Zeek Bey smiled and replied to Gump, "Young brother, I don't mean to break your heart nor hurt your feelings, but I've heard that line before. You're not the original, but I'll give you credit for trying, though." And Zeek Bey ran away with the conversation, "Let's not go global, let's keep it here. We have to learn to bridge the gap between the young and the old. Like the president said to America, we need to help one another. We all need to come together. If you change the language, you can change the mind."

"Man, why'd you wait til you came to prison to get religious?" Jay asked.

"Yeah, that's what we wanna know," Jit said, resting his elbow on Jay's shoulder.

"This is what it took for me to come to my senses," Zeek Bey said, without a mustard seed of shame. "Now I'm aware of my purpose in life. I love helping people; you can't put a price tag on the change that one can make. I'm only here to tell you guys about my change. It's up to you to make that change. I once was rebellious and impatient. Young brothers, there is another percent of prison that is a hell zone. Where I just came from, people just do crazy stuff, giving the administration the green light to hurt them. We must do away with the ignorance; we have to respect one another's differences. President Obama said the right thing is, everybody has to be involved.

We can start right here. Sometimes, people be inductors of what they read. There comes a time in every human life, we must think about others as well. Some people actually think religion is the reason why we can't come together. But me, my brother Shakur, and my other brother Sten X are here to try our hardest to prove them all wrong. When people talk down on someone, sometimes they be just bumping their gums, because you're doing something right or doing something they can't do."

"Man, you know what, you're right, I'm not going to change overnight, but I am going to work towards changing," Gump promised.

"I need to, too," Jay said.

"Boy, it's gonna be hard for us," Jit said, laughing.

Game Tight came around the corner with a grey gym bag of burritos. Zeek Bey always called him 'Get It Right,' because he needed to tighten up and stop lightin' up. The compound had much love for him, he was their chef and always hustling. Another day, another dollar. A day late will definitely be a dollar short. GT was the early bird and always caught the worm.

"ATL's finest," Rail greeted, "You a chef, or a chef's helper?"

"I'ma cut ya toes off! But you don't hear me though!" Black greeted, Game Tight with his very own famous words. Game Tight had everyone saying “I'ma cut ya toes off,” even the officers.

“I'ma cut ya TOES off!” Game Tight hollered, letting everyone know he was on the block with burritos. “I got chicken burritos, they’re full of vegetables, chicken, and cheese.”

“Game Tight, a nigga need to cut ya toes off,” Lloyd said, capping Game Tight.

“Give me foe,” Big said.

“Give me four too,” Peewee repeated.

Game Tight always called Zeek Bey 'Big Homie.' He knew to hold Zeek Bey two book's worth. Zeek Bey always supported everyone’s hustle. “Big Homie, that CO y'all have in y'all’s unit is a fool! You don’t hear me though! One day before the four o'clock count, he was walking around peeking in everybody's windows while holding his keys. He wore a black mask; I thought he was one of the Red Dawgs coming to get me. You don't hear me though! I thought he was coming to cut my toes off.” After Game Tight laughed, he said, “I call y'all’s CO, the Pink Panther by the way, he tiptoed down the range that day.”

Chop walked over. “Game Tight, I need a book's worth.”

“I knew you were coming,” Game Tight lied.

“Every hustler has to respect as well as support the next man hustle.”

“Big Chop gonna always shop with me,” Game Tight said.

He looked into the bag. After the count, there were only eight of them left, and they were for Zeek Bey.

One of Game Tight's young homies came up begging, “Homie, let me get one on my face until I can see better days, come on, throw me one.” He produced both hands as a catcher's mitt.

"I ain't got, but a few and all of them go to the Big Homie," Game Tight replied.

"Man, fuck with a nigga! You know I gotcha!" Young Buck begged again.

Young Buck went in their other homie's unit and saw Nard eating a pizza. He went to begging as usual. Nard told him that he did not eat pizzas and the types of meats he had for toppings. Young Buck assured Nard that he ate everything. Nard told him once again, no he doesn't, because if he did, he'd keep plenty of it.

"I'ma cut ya TOES off!" Game Tight said, to no one in particular.

"Man, there goes the dude they say lucky enough to shit and piss in a hot sauce bottle from a swing set," Young Buck said, while pointing to a guy that he didn't know. Once everyone looked, he stole one of Game Tight's burritos and immediately pocketed it. Zeek Bey walked over.

"Big Homie, I got ya burritos ready for ya!"

Zeek Bey pointed towards Young Buck, "Give the brother one."

"I'ma cut ya toes off," Game Tight said, as he was serving his homie.

"Preciate ya, bruh," Young Buck thanked Zeek Bey.

"God bless ya two times," Zeek Bey said, letting Young Buck know he'd seen him hit the lick. "Man, Game Tight wouldn't give a nigga all the shit he can eat, with his tight ass. He likes to get paid but don't like to pay."

"Game Tight so tight his ass squeaks when he walks. Is that what you're trying to say?" Interjected Slow. "Game Tight, your name should be Ex-lax, cause you get more crap with you then two hog pins."

It wouldn't be laws if there weren't any haters. These

guys would talk behind your back and kiss your tail in public.

"Game Tight, you got any more tasters?" another beggar asked.

"Give him one too," Zeek Bey instructed.

"Thanks, playa."

"I'm just happy that Allah blessed me, so I'm able to be a blessing to others," Zeek Bey said. Game Tight looked back into the bag before handing it over to Zeek Bey. "Big Homie, that's five with the other. I had only seven; I thought it was eight. I got you another one after count, cause I'ma make some more."

"We can say it's eight," Zeek Bey said, ready to pay for the one Young Buck stole. He did not want to see Game Tight take the loss, because not only did he support the hustle, but he respected the hustler.

Mud came under the shed, "I got Oatmeal Pies, Nutty Bars, and M&M's," he said, just naming a few of his items.

"Mud, how them cookies taste?" another youngster asked.

"Delicious!" Mud replied, saying his famous word, which was 'Delicious.' "How them Snickers taste?" another youngster asked.

"Delicious!" Mud rocked.

Mud is a 60-year-old white man. He learned from experience about giving them, youngsters credit.

Now he took to them like a farmer handles his garden. He'd learned how to weed them out, knowing the good ones from the bad, after learning the hard way, which was buying them for 5 dollars.

Mud held a bag of honey nuts in front of Zeek Bey, because he would buy a lot of them from the old head.

"Bruh, feel this bag? This one's heavier than the other

ones," Mud lied and continued to spread his watered-down game SUPER thick. "They put more in this bag than they put in the other bags."

Zeek bey couldn't help but to laugh and go ahead and buy the bag of nuts. "Thanks, Big ZB," Mud said.

Zeek Bey just had to ask, because he enjoyed hearing Mud tell his famous slogan as much as he enjoyed hearing Game Tight say his famous slogan.

"How these nuts taste, Mud?"

"Delicious!"

At USP Petty Rock, there was always violence, madness, and so much tension in the air, but here, they kept Zeek Bey laughing and smiling. These guys were mascots, comedians, and would sell their souls for a Tootsie Roll. They were stamped crazy and there's nothing they wouldn't do for a stamp. What one person wouldn't do, another one will. One fat young guy's famous slogan was "Give me that job that nobody wants." This place was off the chain.

Here and only here these youngsters were still wet behind the ears, still had Similac as well as McDonald's on their breath. They stayed bumping their gums, abusing and misusing the privilege of Freedom of Speech. They stayed talking out the side of their neck, talking just because they had a mouth. Thinking they knew everything, and they thought killers stopped being born after them.

They whined and complained day in and day out. To let them tell it, they had the solution to someone else's problem. They were good for trying to give advice when and where it was not needed, truly just voicing their opinions, since everyone was entitled to one. But they didn't have the formula, medication, or ingredients to their own lives. They couldn't see the bigger picture. They were good for hollering about; they're ready to leave this super, sweet, safe spot and go to the penitentiary.

"I'm ready to go to the USP."

"I can survive behind that wall."

"The penitentiary ain't nothing, the pen ain't ready for me."

The youngsters could have saved their breath. Only a fool would want to put himself in harm's way. Guys in the USP don't want to be there. They would be trying to get their points down to escape the madness, tension, politics, as well as to escape from having to kill or be killed. There's no excuse for ignorance, there's no pass for 'He Didn't Know', or 'Didn't Mean', or 'Meant No Harm or Disrespect.' As the Bible says: Tame the tongue, because that little pink thing is the most dangerous thing on the body. The youngsters were first offenders and would be going against real career criminals.

Zeek Bey closed his eyes and thought of when the youngsters played the old heads in football. USP Petty Rock's field was crowded. Guys were there to entertain and to get entertained. The old heads were doing their thing, but they were no match for the youngsters. The young bucks were too fast and too talented. They stayed 40 to 50 points ahead, and one of the youngsters did too much abusing to the airwaves, with the volume of how an old man can't beat him at nothing. The football field became a crime scene; the youngsters weren't equipped with the USP way of life. The game of sports, a majority of the time, converted into an event of crime scenes and deathbeds.

"Young bucks, y'all ain't ready for them USPs," Zeek Bey shared, "I'm glad to be away from them. I stay on my knees thanking Allah for getting me away from there. I'm tryin' to live to grow old! I don't want to die in jail. The

USPs play for keeps. Stabbing, killing, they stay on lockdown. We get bag lunches for breakfast and dinner. We go to chow only for lunch. Saturday and Sunday, we stay locked down and get bag lunches cause they're short on staff. Sometimes we don't get to go outside but once a week. y'all young bucks know what?"

"What?" the youngest and toughest amongst the group wolfed, because he didn't like anything that Zeek Bey had said.

"A wise man would learn from someone else's experience. He wouldn't have to experience things for them to be his teaching," Zeek Bey enlightened.

"Big Dawg, we wouldn't have to touch the fire to know the fire's hot?" another youngster asked, truly being sarcastic.

"Now you're learning, young grasshopper, "Zeek Bey replied, as he pointed and winked at the youngster who'd spoken.

"I ain't scared of nothing!" The toughest and youngest wolfed.

"Fool, they don't bury the scared, they bury the dead."

Zeek Bey shot the youngster another wink for his wise counseling.

"They can die, too."

"Boy, stop," the wise youngster said, "I'm trying to live. I'm too young to die."

Little did he know, but he'd just set a trend. "Man, I gotta get out of jail and go home, so I can take care of my children and grandchildren."

"My momma and grandmamma gone. I gotta get back there, so I can be there for my auntie."

Zeek Bey now knew he didn't cast his pearls amongst the swine.

---

Zeek Bey always listen to the Tom Joyner show, six days a week, and if he did miss one, it's not going to be on a Wednesday, because they called it, get well Wednesday. A doctor would always be on the show sharing free tips concerning something that consisted of the human flesh. Dr. Amber was discussing hair products causing women, colon cancer and thyroid problems. The blenching of the hair, dying of the hair, and that most women get their hair done at least 3 to 5 times a week. She also stated the chemical harms the little girls at a very young age.

Zeek Bey rubbed over his baldhead and thought, "I'm glad I cut all my hair off because Allah knows I'll still be trying to rock them perms. I don't need them chemicals to destroy my body. Brothers don't go to the doctor as much as they should, we make the greatest mistake by waiting until we get into our 40's when we could've caught the problem or issues when they first develop. Our young males don't visit the doctors, until they come to jail and the people give them a full checkup, such as a colon cancer, cholesterol, prostate cancer, diabetes, high blood pressure, HIV, and any other ailments you may have.

In jail, you're living in the bottom of the society, and you would think it's no way to go but up! But we still have people that amaze me, because they trying to dig that hole deeper. Just when you think it can't get any worse, they'll prove you wrong.

# CHAPTER 12

Shakur was making him, Mr. Ben, and Sten X a seafood spaghetti. He enjoyed cooking and took pride in putting the meals together. Shakur fried the pasta, which he and Mr. Ben preferred. Sten X didn't care how Shakur cooked them, because to him, they both were a tasty dish. The bell pepper, onions, cut up pickles, and vegetable flakes were boiling right along with the mackerel and the smoked clams.

Shakur melted two different pieces of cheese. They would be the sauce.

"Shakur, I wish I knew how to cook," said Sten X.

"I wish you did too, so you'd be doing the cooking today instead of me," Shakur replied, as he poured the noodles equally into their bowls.

"Noodles first," Mr. Ben said.

"Then the meat," Sten X said.

"The cheese sauce last," Shakur lectured.

"That's easy," Sten X predicted.

"The key to cooking is the seasoning," Shakur unfolded.

Sten X watched every move Shakur made, not missing out on a beat. He wanted to learn the cooking techniques. He was always joining Shakur, while he prepared the food.

"I'm getting hungrier, Shakur, while watching you."

"Me too," revealed Mr. Ben, as his stomach began to growl.

"Whose stomach was that?" Shakur asked.

"Mine," Mr. Ben said, being twenty-one .

"It won't be long now," Shakur announced, as he began lacing the top of the spaghetti with the four different kinds of fish. The salmon and oysters were his favorite.

"When my stomach growls, that means it's shrinking," Mr. Ben reminded.

"Yes, sir," Shakur agreed.

"After about six or seven spoons, I'll be full as a tick," Mr. Ben predicted.

"Once the rest of that food marinates overnight," Sten X said, "The next day, it's going to taste even better."

"Always does," Mr. Ben said.

Shakur continued working the task out of habit because he blocked everything out. He did not hear another word Mr. Ben, and Sten X said. He focused on the guys in the unit. The scene did not look right; guys in the same car were doing too much whispering and moving. One guy made the two-man huddle four times, back to back.

Surely, these guys' criminal behavior did not decrease when they came to prison. Their savage mentality wasn't left behind in the society. They talked that talk and were forced to walk that walk. Every single one of them had the same ultimatum: participate with us, or we'll demonstrate, and you'll be our victim as well.

Everyone amongst the car, the circle, had a role to play, knowing they'd have to roll or get rolled on, made them all bring their A-game. This gave the suckers and cowards heart, the opportunity to be a warrior whether he wants to or not. Yes, forcing the gangster or killer label upon one's forehead.

The majority of the guys did not talk that talk but had to walk that walk. No different than the saying, 'You'll make a scared man kill you.' Their variety of leaders, shot-callers, or the voice of the car, whatever title made the car feel comfortable because more often than not, one will say,

"So-and-so is our voice; he's not our shot-caller." You'll also hear, "Bru, don't tell me the problem, take it to our shot-caller."

That individual's not allowing anyone to pin the responsibility on him. Now, not all shot-callers called the shots. He may come to the conclusion of the decision making, but every car will have an arbitrate, that is, if that individual chooses to come forth. The Arbitrate will map out the situation for their soldiers to execute the plan. Everyone not cut from the same cloth to be a soldier, but in the USPs, they'll make one a soldier. One locked up for stealing meat from a grocery store, another for robbing banks with a note, the third guy for a white-collar crime. The word violence never even crossed their vocabulary, but here and only here, everyone will be given a weapon, and one better use it, even though they don't present a dangerous bone in their bodies.

By Shakur being in prison, he was forced to adapt to the environment, and he became a fast learner because, without a survivor kit, one would surely perish. Number one rule: Don't become paranoid, never let them see you sweat, and please, for God's sake, don't be nosy, because if you do one of these, you'll become a certified victim. Shakur was very conservative: the surroundings painted a picture for him, if not to others because not everyone's third eye had or has opened. The guys stuck out like a sore thumb.

"Sten," Shakur whispered.

"What's up bru, what you need me to do?" Sten X asked, ready and willing to wheel to the cell and get whatever Shakur needed.

"Look around the unit… I need to know, do you see what I see?" Shakur instructed.

Sten carried out the mission and shortly said, "All I see is guys watching TV, playing dominoes, and playing chess."

Shakur dismissed Sten X's answer and threw the same challenge to Mr. Ben. "Mr. B, now you do the same and tell me what you see."

"Brother Shakur, I allowed my eyes to roam the unit when you first popped the question to Sten, and I'm still looking, but I see nothing," Mr. Ben said, as he continued looking.

Mr. Ben saw the same events Sten X saw, and nothing different.

"Mr. B, keep looking," Shakur encouraged, expecting Mr. Ben's third eye to be as sharp as his, if not sharper. "Sten, you keep looking, too."

"I never stopped," Mr. Ben stated, as he continued trying to see what Shakur saw, or thought that he saw.

"I am," Sten X informed.

"Everything's sticking out like a sore thumb," Shakur coached.

"What's a sore thumb look like?" asked Sten X.

"Okay," Mr. Ben exhaled, "I see the guy posted by the CO's office."

Shakur looked at his watch, and the guy watching the CO collected the time from him as well, about a few seconds before Shakur, that's what had forced Shakur to follow suit. Shakur began laying out the pieces to the puzzle.

"Mr. Ben?"

"Yes."

"Did you see that guy look at his watch?"

"Shakur, I saw you look at yours, too."

"So what time is it?" Shakur inquired.

"Ten til One."

"Yes, Mr. Ben, ten til One... and I'll say, in about seven more minutes," Shakur predicted.

"Shakur, you're right, that's when shit's going to hit the fan," Mr. Ben agreed, "It's already stinking." Mr. Ben had begun to put the pieces to the puzzle together, and everything stuck out like a sore thumb. Mr. Ben shared all the clues with Sten X, "Brother Sten?"

"Yes, sir?"

"You see the guy watching the CO?"

"Yeah, Mr. B."

"You saw him look at this watch at ten minutes til?"

"Yes."

"Now when I tell you to look, you can't stare. Brother Sten, just steal you a little glance," Mr. Ben instructed. "Slowly cut your eyes to the right, about seven cells down on the bottom range from the front door. There are six guys guarding the cell, and three of them already went into the cell."

"Okay, okay, okay, I can see, I can see, once said the blind man," Sten X said.

Shakur continued getting their food together because he knew it wasn't going to be long before the CO hollered, "LOCKDOWN!" They were on borrowed time, and it all consisted of how that car handled the situation of 'cleaning up' their car, meaning they were going to punish one or two of their homies. The personal beef was within the family, so there wasn't anything that anyone else had to worry about. They were completely free of harm and danger, this time; scot-free.

The architect stayed focused on the officer. As soon as the intercom announced, "Ten minutes, move," the Officer came out and reannounced "Ten Minutes, Move!" for the ones who did not hear the move, so no one was able to say they didn't hear it, or he didn't call it.

As soon as the officer locked his office door, the architect got immediately on his job by secretly and smoothly escorting the officer outside, entertaining him with the conversation of who he thought was going to be the next president. His homies went to work on one of their other homies. The soldiers stabbed him two times a piece, not trying to take his life, but to let him know they meant business. They carried out the assassination because their homie had put his life in danger, by doing not one, not two, but a COUPLE of 'don't-do's.' When these laws are disregarded or disobeyed, there are certain, definitely evil consequences, because one not only brings harm to himself, but to the people around him. It stops one from doing things deliberately or out of ignorance.

The guys exited the building with the rush of traffic, making a smooth getaway. As soon as they reached the bottom step, their victim number two was already heading in their direction without a care in the world. He didn't see it coming until it was too late. They waved him over in a homie greeting, but as soon as he got within striking distance, his homies transformed into demons, swinging with all of their might, face blows. Once his body hit the concrete, they stomped and kicked at him. The pain felt as if they had elephant feet. One of the homies raced off to the softball field, where the game was in motion. He snatched a bat from the next batter up and raced back into their violent circle. His homie was already knocked unconscious, blood escaping from his eyes, ears, nose, and mouth, but he still gave the man a couple of blows to the head. If the tower had dropped the bomb, the victim wouldn't be able to escape the mob with a fighting chance for his life. They had broken all his ribs.

"Get on the ground, now," the intercom erupted, in English and Spanish. The guys dove to the ground, trying to get as far away from their victim as possible, so they'd be able to howl, “It wasn't me!” They would do lots of dumb things but admitting to a crime wasn't going to be one of them.

A variety of staff stormed the rec yard prepared for War or World War II, as they always raced to save a victim or victims' lives. Fifteen staff members were armed with M-16s, taking extra precautions. They knew they were dealing with guys that would take a life at the drop of a hat. Allowing one of the staff to become a victim wasn't in the forecast, as well as becoming a victim themselves.

“Everyone stay facedown until one of my staff gives you a direct order to get off the ground!” a gunman announced.

“Man, the ground's wet!”

“I know it rained, but trust me, the water's not going to hurt you. I have to protect my staff.”

---

Six months after their lockdown, Sten X went to the chapel to watch Hidden Colors. He watched a part every Saturday, until he watched all three parts. Now, he was watching them all over, trying to learn some more knowledge; whatever he wasn't able to digest the first time.

The movie was very educational. Every inmate and convict needed to make it their top priority to invest their time and attention into not one, not two, but all three parts.

Big Buck was in the main chapel with about ten of his Christian Brothers. They were elaborating on a few Bible verses, and Big Buck decided to share with his family the conversation he had with one of the Devil's Advocate.

“The other day, a guy asked me why I smile so much. Why I'm always happy,” Big Buck Began. “I told him, I'm a happy man! I'm not miserable. Some people haven't learned how to do their time, and they're still allowing their time to do them. If they would've watched the TV show called Bretta, Bretta would have told them, don't do the crime, if they can't do the time. I smile so much because Christ is the head of my life. Once they get some Jesus in their lives, they too will be in peace."

"Amen, brother."

"Amen."

"Thank you, Jesus."

"Tell the truth, brother."

"Speak, Big bru, speak."

"Put the alarm clock in the graveyard!"

Big Buck regained control. "If you're a paper chaser, you worship money, that means money is your God. God tells us that if we worship him and do his will, he'll give us a bundle of things. He'll do anything. God is a mysterious God, a loving God, and a forgiving God. God loves the people, and so the people need to give up their sinful ways and show God that they love him as well."

"Preach on, brother, preach."

"You were a student and now you're a teacher."

"Spread God's word!"

"Brothers, if I'm going to be a slave for something, for anyone, then I'm going to be a slave for our merciful Lord. But now, player, we're done converting that word from slave to servant," Big Buck said, smiling.

"A soldier for the Lord."

"God is good."

"ALL the time."

"Use me, my precious Lord."

"You know how they say for the Army, Be all you can be?" Big Buck asked, "Brothers, that's how we have to be for our savior, for our Lord, Jesus Christ. He gave his only begotten son, so we can have what?" Big Buck paused and pointed into their small crowd.

"Eternal life!" they sang out together.

"Jesus died for what?" Big Buck asked.

"For our sins!" they chanted together.

"Then why are we still sinning?" Big Buck asked, then answered himself, "Because we still allow the devil to continue tricking us. I don't know about y'all, but now I'm tired of letting the devil continue to make a fool out of me. He had me like a dog chasing his own tail. My crime days are over. Devil, I rebuke you in the name of Jesus." Big Buck paused to wipe the sweat from his face. "How would you know God's servants?"

"By their actions."

"Their tongue is always speaking the Lord's name."

"That two, and what else?" Big Buck asked.

"They'll walk that walk."

"And talk that talk!"

Big Buck began humming, rocking his head, and snapping his fingers while tapping his feet, and his voice began to surface, "Oh, I've been spreading the news, and if it feels this good being used, you just keep on using me until you use me up."

"Sing, brothers, sing!"

"That's Bill Withers' song," Sten X mumbled and began to sing it himself. "God, if it feels this good being used, Lord continue using me until you use me up."

Big Buck sang the song in church that Sunday, and he got a lot of guys singing alone, and a mighty, miracle occurred. Guys were coming to the altar by the tens, ready to try to be a soldier for the Lord. They wanted some of what Big Buck had and wanted to get a taste of the medication their grandmother had always prescribed for them. They told themselves that Big Momma and Big Buck couldn't both be telling the same lie. Big Buck was one of the Chosen ones and he was blessed with the gift of gab. Everyone always likes him; he was always accepted among any and every circle. When God is with you, no one can be against you. The Big Guy was a living witness.

That night, Big Buck told them,

“Fellows,<br>God hasn't brought us this far to leave us alone.<br>We have to keep the faith<br>and keep the hope alive.”

Time is of the essence. Whatever you do with it, is what you’ll get out of it. Some can put minimum work into it and receive an abundance of wealth or greatness, while others feel that they have to strain to obtain the same results. In life, everything just isn’t meant for some people at that particular time! It’s not meant for one to give up, it’s just that you will probably merely need to change your course of action and thinking. If one is measuring their success and failures based on someone else’s TIME, then they truly haven’t come to understand themselves, because TIME Ends with **ME**!

# CHAPTER 13

Shakur received Reese's mail three days ago, but wouldn't look into the package until today, after he'd prayed asking Allah to remove the anger he had for his cousin. The newspaper clippings were the detectives that bursted him "Now Allah's exposed you devils," he said, while reading over the detectives' charges, "God don't like ugly. Y'all bursted me with my guns. Now y'all get busted with guns. y'all sold my guns and put the weapons back on the street. The same informant y'all used to catch me will now be the informer to testify against you. Now, you detectives didn't know a sword has a double edge? You live by the sword, you die by the same sword. With all these gun charges y'all have, y'all will get to see what it's like to be in a cage," Shakur thought, as he continued looking over the clipping.

Reese kept him updated and promised to do everything in his power to correct the sellout error he had made. "Cuz, a scrambled egg can't be unscrambled, but I can use you and my merciful Lord's assistance, and please, let your detective buddy know my God is powerful."

Shakur saw Stacy heading in his direction. He properly put the clipping back into the envelope.

Stacy wasn't the type of guy he needed to discuss his case with. Shakur would do that only with Reggie. Reggie was the brother with multiple talents. He was the man Allah gave three talents to, because he knew Reggie wouldn't be like the first man and bury the talent. Reggie demonstrated that no different than the second man; he multiplied them. Reggie could sing, play the piano, and the guitar; besides showing off his talents in church, he was a very good lawyer. Reggie always assisted the brothers, even though they were always wearing out their welcome. He was aware that they knew not what they do, so he continued assisting the unappreciative and looked for no reward, because he was content with his blessings coming from God. He's one of God's chosen ones and always spoke highly of God in any and every form of conversation.

"Shakur, peace, bru," Stacy greeted while sitting down at the table with Shakur.

"Peace, bru," Shakur returned the greeting. "So, bru, what brings you outside today?"

"I knew you'd be on the rec yard somewhere, and I wanted to get your input on something," Stacy stated. He would always unload his burden on Shakur, since Brother John sang, *Lean On Me,* in church a few Sundays ago.

"Shakur, I want to talk about some deep shit today."

"Bru, a person who curses is one who has a limited vocabulary. Learn how to talk without the profanity."

"You got that, Shakur."

"So what's troubling you?"

"Shakur, if I didn't get bursted, I would have unintentionally destroyed my whole young generation. I would've been the blind, leading the blind. I was a drug dealer. I would have given my sons that sack, thinking that I would have been assisting them, not knowing that I would be destroying them. I grew up without a father. I did not know how to be a father. I used to hate the guy that set me up. Brother Shakur, if he hadn't set me up, I probably would have overdosed, could have caught AIDS! Be in a grave! Be on death row! So, Brother Shakur, what do you have to say?"

Shakur's mind went into overdrive, because there were avenues he could attack and tackle. "Lil bru, you need to be down on your hands and knees, thanking Allah for being so merciful."

"You're right, Shakur, because now my son is a better man than I am! A better husband than me! A better father than I was, and I thank God for putting me here. So I'll be out of my children's way, and now, they're 100 percent the opposite of me. I did not block the blessing God had for them."

"Stacy, Stacy, Stacy," Shakur whispered, smiling, seeing that the guy had grown because he was able to see his wrongs and admit to his wrongs. Now Shakur had to show Stacy why his prison sentence wasn't a curse but a gift. "Brother, the fact of leaving them at a young age just wears on your mind sometimes, and you're man enough to admit that you failed at parenting. Stacy, Allah puts us here for reasons. Now you'll be able to father, parent, and guide not just your younger generation, but all the young generations as a whole. Brother, Whom much is given, much is required. Allah required you to be fixed, before you could fix the broken fences left behind. Now you know right from wrong, you have a voice. Use that voice to awaken the people and family members. You know the little thoughts that tell you to do this and that?"

"Yes."

"One's the devil, the other one is God," Shakur stated.

"Shakur, I'm not ashamed to admit I'm not as religious as you, so how is it possible for me to know God's voice from the Devil's voice?" Stacy asked, looking confused.

"It's plain and simple, Stacy."

"Speak for yourself."

Shakur began to stroke his beard. "God's voice will not have any sins. Nothing negative. The Devil's voice will always be negative. Telling you to do things you shouldn't do."

"It is easy and simple," Stacy agreed.

Shakur addressed all the issues Stacy stated, but he

refused to speak on anything concerning the guy that set him up. He was grateful that Stacy was able to look deep within his own situation, and see by him coming to prison, that he'd avoided a lot of roads of destruction, because any of those detours meant there was no coming back.

"Stacy, you've opened your eyes and continue to open them more, but only if you learn to love Allah as Allah loves you," Shakur encouraged.

"God is a good God," Stacy stated, "All the time."

"Astaghfirullaaha wa'atoobu'ilayhi," Shakur whispred.

"Shakur, what you just said in Arabic?" Stacy asked.

"I seek the forgiveness of Allah and repent to him," Shakur replied, and said another Arabic sentence, "Subhaan Allaahi wa bihamdihi."

"Shakur, what'd you say that time?" Stacy asked.

"Glory is to Allah and praise is to him," Shakur said. "Stacy, you're not going to remember none of what I just said."

"Tell me a super short one?"

"Allaahu-Ala."

"What's that meaning?"

"Only Allah knows what's best."

"Shakur, I remember you always used to say something else, something like you just said," Stacy said, now actually trying to learn a word here and there like he had learned to speak broken Spanish.

"Allahu-Akbar, what does that mean again?"

"God is great."

"Allahu-Akbar, Allahu-Akbar, Allahu-Akbar," Stacy began repeating over and over. Once he stopped, he'd have the word and meaning a part of his vocabulary. "Allahu-Akbar means God is great."

"Yes, Stacy," Shakur smiled. "Now tell me the other word that I previously gave you that sounds something like Allahu-Akbar."

"That's easy."

"Okay, easy," Shakur replied, as he waved his fingers towards himself, indicating to let him hear it.

"Allahu-Ala."

"Okay," Shakur said, smiling, "What does Allahu-Ala mean?"

"God knows what's best," Stacy said excitedly.

"Only Allah knows what's best," Shakur corrected.

"I was close," Stacy stated. "I said the same thing but needed a little rewording."

"I do not disagree," Shakur said, "They say you'll never know the student's ready until the teacher shows up."

"Man, mothafuckas ain't happy until blood's being shed," a guy said. Truly he was talking about how people play games concerning their debts, with that pet-ta-sweat-ta.

Shakur was glad the guy could see the bigger picture and was able to think outside the box. The guys thought they were doing something slick. The dude was buying them for a little of nothing, all it took was five or ten dollars to keep them out of his face. Lots of guys sell their soul for a Tootsie Roll. They can't get a two-stamp soda on credit, let alone a four-stamp candy bar. "Cash and carry, cause y'all know y'all don't pay. I'ma try to keep y'all's mothers from needing some Paul Barrels." When that guy finished cussing and fussing, he went to walk the track, and Shakur turned his attention to the positive brother, because that negativity wasn't a part of his agenda.

---

Red took a couple of gulps of bottled water. Afterward, he placed the bottle top on Young Big's shoulder. "Put this in your sock, it'll bring you luck," he said, joking.

"I don 't believe in luck," Big replied, truly speaking for the both of them because neither did Red, but he'd always say the word luck came into play when preparation meets opportunity. "I'm blessed every morning I wake up," Big stated.

"You got a little sense, don't you," Red said, smiling, "Even though you don't look like you do." Rock and Big continued to enjoy their game of chess. Big moved his Queen. Red politely intervened with the game by pushing Big's Queen back to the same spot. Big pushed the Queen to the same spot again. Rock took the Queen with his bishop, and Big immediately began whining, "Come on Rock, let me get my Queen back, Red's distracting me."

Rock gave the Queen back because Big couldn't play anything too good, and besides, Rock was just practicing and killing the clock. So why not give the piece back and continue to kill two birds with one stone?

"Big, you say I'm distracting you?" Red asked, "Big man, let me find out you can't chew bubblegum and talk too."

"I already know I can't win," Big admitted.

"Big, you the jack of everything and don't master anything," Red said, laughing.

"Anything," Rock said, laughing.

"Big, you're the Great Bomb," Red said, "And you know it, that's why you named yourself the Great Bomb. You get a shave and haircut, and you'll look like you got some sense."

"That's Big's swag," Rock said. "He's sharper than most twenty-one-year-olds."

Red-spotted Porkchop coming in their direction. "Swag… check out, my big partner… now that's the definition of *swag*."

Everyone turned their attention to the fat white guy, as he cool-daddy walked towards them. He wore a grey fitted cap slightly turned towards the right, a white T-shirt, grey shorts pants, and all-white Air Force Ones.

“What's up, Big Dawg?” Red greeted, giving Porkchop some dap. “Big Dawg Swag, Game #1.”

“Porkchop's a cool white boy,” Big said, “I gotta give him that.”

“Porkchop, I looked in your cell today. I see y'all have a empty bunk. I'ma move over there,” Red said, just talking.

“Come on,” Porkchop welcomed. “You 're one of a few.”

Shakur smiled because the white guy told the brother he was not only welcome to move into their cell with him and his other white celly, but Porkchop stated the brother was one of a few. “Many are called, but few are chosen,” Shakur mumbled. “The brother is a people person; he'll be able to enlighten the people that they can open up doors as well as close doors by how one conducts himself.”

Every person will reveal who they are through their action, speech, and deeds. So watch them very carefully, they’ll give you signs…

The Real
Jay Rock

# CHAPTER 14

"Big Homie, they don't hear me though, you don't hear me though!" Game Tight hollered.

"Game Tight, where's my eight dollars and eight stamps for my two vegetables?" Ro asked.

"I gotcha. I gotcha, homie," Game Tight replied.

"Man, you like to get paid, but you don't like to pay," Ro stated. "And your name ought to be game over."

"Get it right," Zeek Bey addressed Game Tight, because that's the name he'd given him.

"Let me find out you don't like to pay your bills!"

"Mo. Mo," Game Tight asked, "Don't I always pay when I owe?"

"Don't get me to lying," Mo said.

Guys sat around the rec tables, taking turns telling Game Tight that they were going to cut his toes off.

"Get it right, if you owe the man," Zeek Bey encouraged, "then pay the man. Bru, you're a businessman! You lead by example. You're out of all people who don't need nobody to holler about you owe them some money."

"You right, you right, Big Homie," Game Tight replied to Zeek Bey, and he paid on the bill and not off the bill. Now his tap was down to eight dollars, which he'll drag and spin his homie for another couple of weeks.

"Zeek Wilson, report to the Lieutenant's Office immediately. Zeek Wilson, report to the Lieutenant's Office immediately." The intercom announced.

"Big Homie, they called your name twice, so whatever it is, it's gotta be something important," Game Tight said.

He was truly, glad they called Zeek Bey to the Lieutenant's Office, because now he wouldn't have to give him a free piece of cheesecake, that he'd made out of butter pecan ice cream. Game Tight wanted to sell Zeek Bey a slice in the first place. He was good for hollering that all the free samples were gone.

Once Zeek Bey reached the LT's office, his counselor and Unit Manager were present.

"Zeek Wilson, please state your name and number," asked the female LT.

Zeek Bey looked at them all as if they were insane, because his Unit Team knew he was himself, live and in the flesh, but he went ahead and executed the direct order. Once he was finished, the LT looked from her personal ID card of him.

"Zeek Wilson, today is your lucky day. The courts vacated the rest of your sentence. Today, you become a free man. You have one hour to be out of our institution. The next bus leaves out within two hours from now. You go straight to your unit, get your property together, and be back up here within 30 minutes. That is if you want to go home."

Zeek Bey became discombobulated once she mentioned the word "Freedom." The case Buck filed for him had set him free. The same thing that made him cry was now making him laugh. The courts had done the right thing by correcting their wrongful "justice." The female judge had departed from the guidelines. She'd sentenced Zeek Bey out of emotion; she allowed her feelings to interfere with her line of duty and seeked to punish him, because she had the authority. She felt Zeek Bey's pregnant victim's pains and set out to torture him in every form and fashion within her power.

"Zeek Wilson, what do you have to say?" asked his counselor.

"This is God's work," Zeek Bey confessed.

"Yes, God is still in the blessing business," stated the Unit Manager.

"Wilson, you can go on back to the unit and get your stuff together, so we can get you out of here and to the bus stop," said the female LT.

"I'm already ready. I stay ready to keep from having to get ready," Zeek Bey said, without blinking an eye.

The Lieutenant thought he was just bumping his gums, but he was serious as a heart attack. Thirty-five minutes later, Zeek Bey was in the prison van, heading for the bus station. The officer driving decided to converse with Zeek Bey, to see if he was going to be another inmate to use the prison system as a set of revolving doors.

"Wilson, you know we're going to leave the light on for you because we know that you'll be back," the officer claimed.

"You're a lying ass," Zeek Bey stated.

"Wilson? You know so many guys have sat in that same seat and said they weren't coming back, and they came back," the officer restated his fact, as he looked into his rearview mirror because he wanted to see Zeek Bey's facial expression.

"CO, man, ain't no women here, and besides, I don't lie to myself, so why do I have to lie to you?" Zeek Bey stated, looking into the officer's rearview to lock eyes with him. "Bru, being in prison means that I'm limiting myself. I'm giving up worldly privileges. Now, that doesn't sound logical to a wise man. Maybe to a damn fool. The people tell you when to shit, shower, and shave.

In prison, y'all aren't called guards, y'all are originally called overseers. I've had enough of the slavery. Yes sir, my slavery days are completely over."

"I like that, Wilson," the officer said, as he felt Zeek Bey's pains, "Honestly, I never looked at it like that."

"Now don't get me wrong, I learned a lot in prison, because God intervened in my street propaganda, and sat me down, as well as opened my eyes to life in general. Now I can see the bigger picture."

"God intervened again and vacated the rest of your sentence," the officer said.

"God wants me to take my show on the road. God's still working with me, but now I'll go home and share the knowledge, the understanding, and the wisdom." Zeek Bey said, as he continued looking into the officer's rearview mirror.

"Good luck, Wilson, but them youngsters out there ain't trying to hear nothing nobody has to say. You know if they're not listening to their parents, their not going to listen to nobody else. Bru, now they're jumping out of the womb killing. All them youngsters got guns bigger than me and you both, and they're not afraid to use them. They'll kill you for looking at them wrongly. I stay the hell out of their way, out of their lane."

"I'm a firm believer. CO, man, there's no such thing as L-U-C-K. Whatever happens to me was my destiny, whether good or bad and besides, my trials and tribulations were the ingredients needed to make me the man I am today. Whatever you like baking, bread, cookies, cakes, you have to use the right ingredients."

"Alright ingredients," the officer said interrupting Zeek Bey's sentence.

"Now, Bru, I'm a soldier for the Lord. Yes, I'm tired of performing as though I'm a dog running around in a circle chasing it's own tail." Zeek Bey continued.

Once they reached the bus station, the CO advised Zeek Bey that he could fool himself, and he could fool him, but no one could fool God. He also told Zeek Bey that he wished him all the joy and success that the world had to offer.

Zeek Bey had thirty minutes before his bus arrived. He thought about where he'd come from, afterward, he thanked God.

"God, thank you for the second chance. Thank you for teaching me there's no such thing as too late... Every time they had me standing on that black box, shackled, I felt like a slave. I'd be so humiliated; I would want to cry. And every time they made me get naked… I've had to stand there naked before them and follow their instructions. Open your mouth, run your fingers through your hair, hold up your testicles, pull the skin back. Now turn around, spread both butt cheeks, bend over, squat and cough, hold up both feet, so I can look under the bottom of them…"

An older lady sitting next to Zeek Bey brought him back to reality.

"Is everything alright, young man?"

"Yes, why do you ask?"

"Because you're crying, son."

Zeek Bey was embarrassed for crying in public. He accepted some tissue and wiped away the tear.

"I'll never go back," he mumbled.

"Young man, whatever problems you have, give them to God. God is a mystic God, and can perform miracles."

"I'm a living witness," Zeek Bey proudly stated.

"You too?" the elder spoke from experience as well. "Young man, you must be one of the Chosen Ones, to learn about the Lord within a young age. Son, God has great, big plans for you," She shook that favorite finger at Zeek Bey. "You mark my words."

"Yes, ma'am."

"I'ma pray for you son."

"Thank you."

"You know, prayers changes things."

"Ma'am, I'm a firm believer."

Mrs. Jones' strong words of wisdom gave Zeek Bey the strength that was needed because his mother and grandmother both had passed away while he was in the servitude condition.

# CHAPTER 15

Big Ro invited Lawyer Corn to his mansion, which sat on ten acres. The Kingpin's land consisted of a compound. He had a fitness center, spar, inside tennis court, basketball court, pool, studio, three live-in five-star chefs, and seven maids. Corn fell completely in love with the Royal Treatments. Big Ro advised him to utilize his baby palace as if it was his own. The lawyer enjoyed the grand tour of the wine cellar. He sipped out of bottles that he could not pronounce the names of. Corn was swept off his feet. The two-day vacation gave him a beautiful taste of the life-styles of the rich and the famous.

Once he explored the ship, his wife manifested that she could live in the yacht for the rest of their lives, because the yacht was equipped with the same activities as Big Ro's palace, if not more. Ms. Corn went jet-ski riding and deep-sea scuba diving. The luxury lifestyle was mindblowing for them both. Every one of the employees showed them so much love and respect. They catered to all of their wants and needs. The couple was treated as if they were Big Ro's mother and father.

The lawyer emerged around in a thin white robe, smoking expensive cigars as he constantly kept his throat wet with 1404 bottles of wine. Big Ro looked at his watch; the Kingpin's timepiece was something you would find in the Rob Report Magazine.

*I have given him a world of pleasures. Now it's time to get down to business*, Big Ro thought to himself. Besides, that was the only reason for him being here.

"Knock, knock?"

"Yes," Big Ro said, as he paced around his library,

"Please enter."

"Sir, is there anything I can do for you?" A beautiful maid stepped forward.

"As a matter of fact, yes, there is," Big Ro said, as he snapped his fingers. "Would you please be so kind as to tell Mr. Corn that I'm waiting in the library for him?"

"Yes, sir."

"And would you please be kind enough to escort him to me? Because we wouldn't want him to get lost, now would we?" Big Ro said as he held up a finger.

"No sir, we wouldn't want that to happen, sir."

"Thank you."

"Sir, it will be my pleasure, sir."

Before Precious could close the door, Big Ro gave her another assignment. "One more thing, please?" Precious paused and did a spin on her right foot, so she'd be facing him once again. "I would like a bottle of wine from the year of 1300 for this occasion."

"Yes, sir."

Precious delivered Big Ro's message to the lawyer first, and as she expected, he needed about twenty minutes to get himself together, which was perfect timing, because that gave her the time needed to go to the wine cellar. Big Ro had not once complained about her choice of taste. He never failed to compliment Precious for her selection.

Around forty-two minutes later, there was a polite knock on the library door. "Knock, knock?"

"Please enter," Big Ro said, as he slipped out of the comfortable chair.

The lawyer entered with Precious trailing him. She was carrying a silver tray containing two wine glasses, the bottle of wine Ro requested, and a bucket of ice. Precious placed the tray on the coffee table and immediately, silently exited the library, giving the gentlemen privacy.

"Mr. Corn, I would like to thank you for accepting my invitation," Big Ro said, smiling.

"My wife and I are very pleased for you to invite us into your world of the world," the lawyer said, as they shook hands. "I must admit, your place is what I'd call heaven on Earth."

Big Ro smiled. "Now Mr. Corn, speaking of a world into another world, I have something that I need to get your expectation on." He retrieved the remote and aimed it towards his 82-inch flat-screen television.

Mr. Corn invested his interest in some of the expensive paintings that decorated the room. "Mr. Ro, I see you're into painting. Are you a collector?"

"No."

"You have some beautiful paintings here!" Mr. Corn said, wishing he had the cost of a couple of the paintings in his bank account. "Jesus."

"Yes, I must admit, they are beautiful and breath-taking," Big Ro said. He loved the sense of power that the paintings always brought him. "Mr. Corn, believe it or not, I got all of them babies at a steal. I mean at a VERY good discount. A very good friend of mine informed me that he had a large collection of exclusive paintings."

"Good God," Mr. Corn exhaled, as he continued to praise the collection. "How much are they worth, a mil, maybe two mil total?"

"Actually, they're worth two million and some change, but as I previously stated, I got them for a steal," Big Ro said, as he looked into Mr. Corn's facial expression. He'd already went over hills with the paintings. "I gave a million in cash for them all. The guy was down on his luck."

"I would have been obliged to do the same as you, especially if I was able and in your position."

A friend of a friend notified Big Ro that he could buy

the stolen paintings half price, and in return be rewarded with double his investment, but since the paintings got so much praise, he had decided to keep them. Besides, they don't lose value. They only increase.

The painting was the last thing on Big Ro's mind. He was ready to get to his top priority. “Mr. Corn, please take a seat and make yourself comfortable,” Big Ro waved towards his luxury sofa and chair. Once the lawyer was seated, Big Ro brought the screen to life, hoping to share his pains. “I have watched this over a million times,” he unconsciously said, while fixing himself a drink.

Mr. Corn watched with disbelief as Sten, and the detective had the shootout. As soon as Sten's pants began to ease down his small waist, Mr. Corn knew he was doomed. Each time the detective fired into Sten's body, the lawyer blinked. As Sten's body was falling to the concrete, Mr. Corn emerged from his soft seat. He watched with disbelief as the detective walked up to Sten's unconscious body, kicking the weapon from his loose grip, and retrieving the other gun Sten had dropped. The detective knelt beside Sten’s head. “You fucking nigga,” he growled, and put the pistol to Sten's head and pulled the trigger. Mr. Corn continued to watch in silence as Big Ro's Bentley sped down the road in 3-D to rescue Sten. Big Ro exited from the back seat. “That's my son, that's my son!” He raced to Sten and also knelt, taking Sten's hand as Big Ro watched his other hand ease underneath his shirt, then he turned off the screen.

“Mr. Corn, would you like a glass of wine?” Big Ro washed down his glass and was getting ready for a refill.

“Sure, why not. I could use a drink right about now,” the lawyer said, wiping a hand over his face. “How long have you had this video?” he asked while receiving the glass of wine. "Thank you," he mumbled, as he accepted it.

Big Ro had a camera in his front and back tag, taking extra precautions in case one of his enemies or jack boys tried to tail him, which never took place. Now, the cameras had finally served their purpose.

"I have cameras in my tags." Big Ro took a couple of quick swallows from his glass. "Mr. Corn, do you have any kids?"

"A son and a daughter."

"Sten is all I have."

"I see where you're going," Mr. Corn said, draining his glass. He was abreast beforehand concerning Big Ro's issue, but the video was a total surprise… or his partner at the firm had failed to bring it to his attention, which he seriously doubted because the video alone was a key piece of evidence.

"How far are you willing to go with this?" the lawyer asked, as he put a hand over his face and massaged both of his temples.

Mr. Corn felt the need to re-word his sentence, because his hindsight had kicked in, producing another clear picture of a flashback when Big Ro's right hand went underneath his shirt. If the police cars would have been only a few seconds late, there would have been no need for his assistance. It was no secret that Big Ro was a criminal, and very heavily into the life of crime… as well as the fact that it was no secret that Mr. Corn loves money and had a luxury lifestyle. He took on only the big buck clients, six figures and better. To catch his attention, throw a dollar sign into the air. He was going to move that mountain case that burdened his clients, or he was going to move that mountain to seize the bundle out of their pockets. He too was a crook and was going to go that extra mile. He took pride in his job, in his work. There were no limitation that can be measured that he wouldn't take to win a case. Clients with long papers, deep pockets activate his criminal mind and keep his wheels turning.

"Mr. Ro, this is a very, very interesting case. This case can make headlines with that video if I can pull the right strings."

"I have faith in you, Mr. Corn."

"Mr. Ro, I take accountable that many uncountable bills have been passed through-"

Big Ro cut the lawyer off. "You don't have to go there," Big Ro smiled, "All you have to do is tell me the figures, and we can seal the deal."

"Mr. Ro, what I'm trying to say is… have you ever took the time out to examine or read the words that are engraved on the back of the greenback bills?"

"Yes?"

"What's back there?"

"Are you talking about In God We Trust?"

"Absolutely."

"You ready for another drink?" Big Ro asked as he was in the process of fixing himself another drink. "The wine helps to ease my mind."

"Mr. Ro, I'm going to put my all into this case, by all means necessary. Are you a praying man?"

"Yes," Big Ro confessed truthfully, as he removed one of his expensive cigars from the box. He clipped one end and put fire to it. After filling his lungs with smoke, he exhaled. "I have a little bit of faith."

"The Bible clearly stated, all we need is faith the size of a mustard seed."

"You think you can win this case?"

"I can't guarantee it, but it looks pretty good in our favor, because the detective did too much. I mean, by him saying the "N-word"! Shooting your son in the head while he was already in a critical condition, and he shot the victim with his own weapon. It's possible the detective could have gunned down his partner with the same weapon. Mr. Ro, let's just hope and pray that the detective's deceased partner's body had the same bullet shells as our victim. Mr. Ro, please do keep in mind that all it takes is one. One shell, Mr. Ro., one shell."

"I'll keep my fingers crossed," Big Ro said, clinking glasses with the lawyer.

Seven-piece conversation to the beast:
we losing our youth is a serial epidemic
I now named this, my 7th amendment.

I know this isn't what you want, but what you need
I'm talking to the last of the dying breed

Them USP's ain't playing no games, all of 'em off the chain
Designed for a duration for us to remain

I'm talking out of love, what's been placed on my heart
From our Father from up above, cause we all must pass on the love

This content is not to be sugar-coated nor glorified
A wake-up call for the youth to start to value their freedom and precious lives

Let's state facts; the system is filled with black
We are repeated offenders (revolving door), we keep coming back
Thinking we can't do jack, but slang that iron and pimp that sack

It’s sad but something serious, it’s not too late
to take Michal Jackson's advice, by making that change
with the man you see, when you look into your mirror

One is one’s own worst enemy, only the wise ones will
agree
People, get under some kind of religious umbelly
Then, and only then, we will be able to come together

# CHAPTER 16

Today was a busy day. The new guy went to the cell the officer assigned him to. Urkel was standing on a chair taking his clothes off of the top shelf. The new guy knocked on the door, before entering the cell and said, "Bruh, I'm your new celly. I just got off the bus."

"How much time you got?" Urkel began interviewing the new guy.

"Two years, I'm back on a violation."

"Where you from?"

"Birmingham."

"What's your name?"

"Damage."

After the new guy stated his name, he watched Urkel stuff his clothes into the laundry bag.

"Bruh, you my celly?"

"Naw, I'm moving. That was your celly that just walked out of here."

Damage looked back at the brother who was his celly, but his celly was racing out the door, trying to make it to Rec before the move closed, so Damage turned his attention back to Urkel as he continued packing his property.

"Damage, you're not going to like your celly," Urkel began to drop salt.

"Why not?"

"Because he's been locked up a long time," Urkel revealed, "He's been down for over two decades!"

"That's why you're moving?" Damage asked.

"I can't live with him no more," Urkel stated. "He does

too much shit. He doesn't leave the cell. He stays in the room all day."

"What he be doing?" Damage asked, looking puzzled, because he wanted to know beforehand what he was walking into.

"All kinda stuff," Urkel said, "You'll see."

"Man, you finished over there by the bed? Cause I had a long ride, and I'm ready to lay down," Damage said.

The 4 a.m. wake-up, preparing for transfer, going through all of the B.O.P. hula hoops wore him down. A few hours of rest would do his body some good.

Once the next ten-minute-move was announced, Damage abandoned the bunk, because he wanted to locate his cousin, who'd been incarcerated for over a decade.

During the 4 o'clock count, Damage small-talked with his celly. Conscious took him to meet his homies as well as to his cousin's unit. Everyone told him great things about his celly.

"Conscious is your celly?" Foe Ya Pleasure asked Damage.

"Yes."

"You in there with a good man," Foe Ya Pleasure said, and continued to speak highly of him.

One of Damage's homies saw him with Conscious. "Homie, you're walking with a good man, and he's one hundred. He's a good dude, and he doesn't deal with too many people. I don't see him as much as I used to."

The next day, Urkel asked Damage, "You've seen it yet?"

"Seen what?" Damage asked. "What am I supposed to see?"

"See what he's doin'?"

"I ain't seen nothing," Damage stated with an attitude. "What's the man be doing?"

"You'll see," Urkel said.

The day after, Urkel questioned Damage again.
"You haven't seen it yet?"
"Seen what?"

Urkel still wouldn't say, he just continued heading for the front entrance, so he could go to the slave factory, because that was his only income. Urkel poured salt on Conscious' character to any and everybody who would listen. Urkel was the king of gossip. Always in the CO's office or standing outside talking to him, which is a validation of the Convict Code. He hadn't been on the compound long, and he knew more people than Conscious. Little did Urkel know, the individuals would tell Conscious everything Urkel would say. They knew why Urkel didn't like Conscious, because Conscious would eat and wouldn't break bread, nor would Conscious serve him, and it hurt Urkel's heart that he had to get other customers to shop with his celly for him.

Urkel had been incarcerated for a decade and some change. If he would have brought whatever was destroying him to Conscious' attention, communication and understanding, which is the best thing all around the world. Urkel wasn't telling the story right. When he first stepped foot on the compound, he was trying to get to know everybody. He supported Conscious' hustle but continued to spin him about the ten dollars. Conscious wasn't tripping, but he kept his ear to the ground. Urkel saw Conscious talking to one of his homies and walked into their presence and rudely said, "Conscious, you know my people?"

"This is my homie," Conscious replied.

Urkel had been on the compound for a few days, and he watched how people respected Conscious, so he tried very hard to tie into Conscious, but Conscious knew Urkel was too friendly and loved to talk. So Conscious wasn't trying to get to know him. Conscious went to the hole four months later, and when he got out, they put him in the cell with Urkel.

Conscious tried to give a guy 50 dollars to switch cells, and the guy was going home in ten or twelve days. The guy was broke and doing bad, but he wouldn't be Urkel's celly, and he needed that money worse than a hog needs slop.

“Don't nobody want to live with Urkel,” Urkel's best friend stated.

Urkel had been incarcerated for over a decade and came from another USP. He came here with no property. No shoes, no sweats, no shorts, no nothing. He'd been on the BS. His homies in his car had robbed him and checked him in, is the conclusion that everyone came to. Urkel didn't even have a bowl to eat out of. He asked Conscious to let him use a bowl, but Conscious declined and later allowed him to use the bowl. Urkel returned the bowl, but it wasn't the same one Conscious had let him use, so Conscious told him to keep the bowl. Urkel had hyena in his DNA; once the park went hunting, he felt he had the right to eat, too.

Now to answer the question of what Conscious had been doing, He stayed in the cell writing to secure his future. He didn't live up to Urkel's expectations by breaking bread. He did not entertain Urkel's BS, because he wasn't on “little boy's” time. He stopped talking to Urkel, period because they were on different levels. He didn't cook with Urkel and wouldn't loan Urkel anything. Urkel was deeply assaulted, because they were under the same religious umbrella. Conscious knew Urkel was faking it to make it. Urkel always talked that tough-man talk amongst his circle, but he knew better than to try Conscious because Conscious told him from day one that he'd assaulted over a dozen of his cellies and when that door locked, that's the time for his cellies to try their luck, if they felt lucky. Conscious learned early in his bid not to take nothing personal of what his celly or cellies did, because he was doing his time and could care less what other people do or don't do.

Urkel took a year and split it in half, and spent the first six months minding his own business and spent the other six months staying out of everybody else's business.

Conscious sat at the rec table discussing the issue with his soldiers. “This clown-ass lil boy keeps talking about me behind my back. He's doing what women do, I’m sorry, but I can’t be his babysitter, his yes man. I refuse to drop to his level, and inherit his character.”

“Big bru, lil buddy don’t mean no harm. He's wise enough to know that barking up your tree is like playing Russian Roulette with all six bullets in the chamber,” Jason stated. “He's just doing what he does. He's loquacious.”

“Very talkative,” Car Wash stated, saying the meaning of 'loquacious.'

“Boy, you’re done losing over two years of good time already, for shedding these suckers' blood. You forgot they're called 'time stretchers?'.” Larry stated, “You gave them that name.”

“This is his way of trying to be your friend,” Car Wash said. “Because he know’s you’re a good person. This is the only route he knows.”

“Big bru, if you sit back and analyze the situation, you know that kid don't mean any harm. You and I both know that he's just faking it to make it. Bru, you going to get mad at this Urkel-looking mothafucka? He's a clown, a mascot! He gossips more than women, and he loves attention. Always wants to be the center of attention. Big Bru, check yourself before you wreck yourself,” Lucky said. “Big Homie, it's impossible for anyone to get mad at

Steve Urkel, because Urkel is gonna be Steve Urkel. If anything, you need to thank him for getting on out of your way."

"You remember he told you he was going to stay away from Young Munchy, Cause Young Munchy be talking crazy to him? The lil boy told you in so many words that he doesn't want any problems," Car Wash said. "Urkel's always Big Boy Wolving. I ain't asked him how many bodies he's got, or how many people he's shot, or how far his chest sticks out. He'll be talking like that because he doesn't want nobody to test their waters. He'll be capping like he's gonna be the suspect, but when the shit's all over, he is going to be the victim, stating he hit me first."

"He's supposed to be too intelligent to be gossipin', people held him for higher standards, he's still lost in his ignorance. Every Zebra will show its stripes," Conscious stated.

"Bruh, if Car Wash is able to identify this lame, then so should you," said Larry.

"Nobody can get mad with Steve Urkel; he's here to keep us laughing instead of crying," Sneak stated. "Everybody does their bid off of him. You see, the COs love to see his good-talking ass coming because he's going to help them do their eight hours. Conscious, the boy far from intelligent. A wise man can play the fool, but the fool can't play the wise man."

Shakur had been sitting at the next table. He overheard their conversation, and knew that Conscious was a good brother, an intelligent brother, and had far too much to lose by going out like a sucka. Urkel was a crash dummy, and would soon crash on his own, because he stayed in other peoples business, stayed doing all of the wrong things, and most of all, no one wanted to be his broke-ass celly. Shakur watched the time from his watch ten minutes before the move. He was posted by the gate, waiting for Reggie to enter, so he could discuss his case and see if Reggie had time to file the motion he needed.

Shakur walked over to the group of guys. “How you good men doing today?”

“Shakur, what's up big bru?” Jason said, while saluting Shakur.

“What's up, Shakur?” Car Wash greeted.

“We're blessed and highly favored, Brother Shakur,” said Larry.

“Peace and love, Brother Shakur?” Sneak greeted.

Conscious shook Shakur's hand and gave him a brotherly hug and said, “Everything's good beloved. How are you?”

“Conscious, can I get a few minutes of your time?” asked Shakur.

“Sure, no problem, big bru,” Conscious said, walking away from the group with Shakur.

Once they were off to the side by themselves and no one could easedrop, Shakur mumbled just loud enough for Conscious to hear. “A 'oothu billahi min ash-shaytaa nir-rajeem.” Conscious was no stranger to the Arabic language; he knew a lot of the Muslim words, even though he did not use them. “I seek refuge in Allah from Satan, the Outcast,” he said in English.

Shakur needed those words to roll off of Conscious' tongue to put him back into the remembrance of Allah. Shakur laid his right hand on Conscious' shoulder. “Lil brother, sometimes, one can be one’s own worst enemy. The old you is fighting the new you.”

Conscious looked away from Shakur and rubbed over his face because he knew these words, as well as the fact that he'd allowed the devil to slightly take control.

“Satan, the devil, is still trying to steal your blessings.

Still trying to keep you and all of us from thinking outside the box. To keep us from actually seeing the bigger picture. Once one begins to put in work for the devil," Shakur paused, to shake his head from left to right. "He doesn't want to lose you. Satan is trying to hold onto you, lil brother. You have to do the driving, because we can't afford to allow Satan, the Devil, to drive for us, because if we do, he'll take us where he wants us to go. You need a designated driver, brother?" Shakur asked, looking him deeply into the eyes.

"Satan can't drive for me anymore, beloved."

"Conscious, it previously sounded like he was. So lil brother, that's why I pulled you over, so that I can be your designated driver."

"I wasn't thinking, Shakur," Conscious sadly admitted.

"I called these cells, cages," Shakur began, "And brothers fight about a cage. A cage that the government got you locked in. Now you're fighting to stay in that cage, instead of assisting each other to fight to get out of these cages. Lil brother, the brothers must understand that we're conducting a war against each other instead of a campaign to win our freedom. Wars end, but campaigns last forever. Campaigns are ongoing, they never stop. So let's end this war amongst each other and conduct this campaign for our liberty."

"Insha-Allah," Conscious said, meaning If it is the will of Allah.

"Allahu-ala," Shakur stated.

"Yes, beloved," Conscious agreed, and said the Arabic words in English, "Only Allah knows what is best."

"Stay focused, lil brother. Don't allow anyone or anything to get you sidetracked. Stay in your lane and on your square," Shakur advised.

After they did the brotherly hug and were shaking

hands, Conscious recited, “Bismillaah. Astagh- firullasha wa'atoobu ilayhi. A 'hamdu lullaah. Laa'ilaaha 'illallaah, allaahu 'akbar.”

“Yarhamullallaah,” Shakur said, meaning “May Allah have mercy upon you.” The Arabic that Conscious had recited said:

In the name of Allah,
I seek the forgiveness of Allah and repent to him.
All praises and thanks are to Allah.
There is none worthy of worship but Allah,
for Allah is the greatest…
God is Good.

When Conscious returned back to his homies, Car Wash was braiding Special's hair. He was jamming somebody's mp3. “Conscious, I'm listening to 2 Chainz, and he just spits a powerful verse.”

“What he said?” Conscious asked.

“If I kill you, I'm famous, and if you kill me, you brainless,” Car Wash said, as he worked.

“So what you're tryin' to say is, if Urkel knocked me off, he's famous, and if I knock him off, I'm brainless?” Conscious asked, with a smile.

“Exactly,” Car Wash replied.

“I thought Jay-Z said that?” asked Jason.

“I just heard 2 Chainz say it,” Car Wash said.

“Well Car Wash, I'm going to give you the credit, because that was one of your purposes in life….. to relay that message to me,” Conscious said.

A couple days later, the compound changed Steve Urkel name to Amtrak, because they knew he was bound to derail. Amtrak started a fight with a scary dude, and the dude beat him. Almost knocked him out. Steve Urkel, A-

K-A Amtrak, fight game was straight zero, now to everyone he's just another mascot, a complete j-o-k-e.

Shakur and Reggie finally got together. Once he showed Reggie the clipping out of the newspaper, Reggie advised him that he'd file a motion on his behalf, and he should be on the first thing smoking back home to his family.

"Brother Shakur, you got yourself something right here. This here is your loophole. How can they argue with your case, especially when their law enforcers are dead in the wrong?" Reggie stated, as he took another long look at the detectives and the guns. "Big brother, this is a beautiful picture the newspaper printed."

"A'hamdu-lillaah," Shakur whispered. "All praise be to Allah."

"God is good, ain't he?" Reggie stated.

"This was the decree of Allah," Shakur stated, giving God credit.

"I'm a firm believer, brother Shakur," Reggie agreed. "This is God's work, and God doesn't like ugly. God takes care of his people. The people can give us this time, but God can say and do something differently."

---

FREE ADVICE
CONTINUE TO PRAY,
GOD GOT YOU…

# CHAPTER 17

Shakur's Mother, Annie, had her face buried into the Qu'ran, immediately after she finished offering salat. She offered du 'aa for Shakur on a daily basis. Annie stayed in Allah's ears, begging for the mercy of her oldest child. Annie also encouraged Shakur's baby brother to pray for Shakur, asking Allah to forgive Shakur of his wrongdoing.

The phone rang, and Shabazz wasn't home to answer it. Annie read way over the daily portion, so she closed the Qu'ran, calling it a quit for the day, and decided to answer the phone.

"Hello?" she said politely.

"This is a prepaid call coming from a Federal Correctional Institution. Caller, please state your name," the machine said. "Shakur Douglas," she heard her son say his name. "If you wish to accept this call from this caller, please push five now, or to-"

Annie intruded into the program's message by pushing the number five. She did not care to hear all of the other options; she didn't want to prolong herself from hearing Shakur's voice any further than absolutely necessary.

"As-Salaamu' Alaikum, son."

"Wa 'alaikum-as-salaam, Mother."

"Shakur, how's everything going?"

"A'hamdu lillaah."

"Do they feed y'all good in there?"

"A 'hamdu lillaah."

Annie knew that Shakur wasn't going to complain about anything; that's why he continued saying "A'hamdu lillaah," which meant all praise be to Allah. No matter how hard, rough, or bad that things may seem, Annie and her family had always turned to God, asking for assistance and for his mercy. God was the answer to all of their problems, and they always called on him, even when good things happened to them as well.

"Momma, I just filed on a few issues concerning my case. The brother who assisted me says everything looks good in my favor, Insha-Allah."

"Insha-Allah," his mother repeated, knowing that nothing in life happened, unless it is the will of Allah.

He didn't go far into the details of his case, because his mother was ignorant to the law, and he did not want to spend their fifteen-minute call breaking down his case to give her a full understanding.

"Allahu-ala," Annie said, meaning Allah is the best of planners. She then began to try to speak things into existence. "This is your year, son. You've done your time. They gave you all of that time, and you didn't kill anybody."

Shakur took full control of the conversation, because he did not want or need his mother to get upset. He just wanted her and his baby brother to be the very first people that he shared the good news with.

"Mother, I thank Allah that I'm here, because now Allah has opened my eyes to a lot of things. Also, I'm now able to see the bigger picture. I'll do better by you and by Shabazz."

"You need some money, son?"

"No. Keep your money, Mom. Allah is my provider," Shakur stated. He did not want to accept his mother's hard earned money, because she and his little brother could put the money to better use. The system gave him three hot meals daily. He was healthy as a horse and in his right frame of mind. Shakur was an entrepreneur, and he knew how to live off of the land and how to make a dollar out of fifteen cents.

"Son, I love and miss you."

"I love and miss you as well, Ma."

"Me and Shabazz always make du'aa for you."

"Thank you, Ma."

"What else can I do for you, son?" she asked, because Shakur would not let her send him anything nor do anything for him. Shakur did not want to put any extra pressure on her, because he was aware that life was hard with her being a single parent and trying to make ends meet. Annie's piece of job was not paying too good. His brother was in the eighth grade, 6 foot 2, wearing a size sixteen shoe, and was steadily growing. His mother was always talking about how he's always outgrowing his clothes, needing more clothes and more shoes, and eating her out of a house and home.

"Ma, I have a few extra dollars. I'm going to send you a couple of dollars," Shakur said, as he was squeezing some lime juice into his bottled water.

"Keep your money, Shakur, I'm alright."

"I'm going to send it to you anyway," Shakur said, taking a super-large swallow from his water bottle. "You can use the three hundred to help you with a bill or two."

"My bills are alright, son. Allah makes sure we got a roof over our head, food, and plenty of running water." Shakur laughed.

"What you laughing for, boy?"

"Because I inherited your stubbornness," Shakur said. "Ma, I'm sending you the money. Now, whatever you choose to do with it is your choice."

Annie exhaled. "I guess I'll buy your brother a few pairs of pants and another pair of shoes."

"A'hamdu Lillaah," Shakur mumbled.

"Shakur, I can tell that Allah's been working with you. I can hear it in your voice."

"Yes. Allah is increasing me with knowledge."

"I always prayed, and still pray to this very day, asking Allah to strengthen you and Shabazz."

"I always pray for guidance, Ma. I also asked Allah to guide Shabazz as well, because I don't need Satan to trick him into making a mistake as I have. All it takes is one mistake for one to lose their life or freedom. These people have no problem with burying you alive." Shakur continued explaining to his mother about how beautiful that Allah was to him, because that was their type of language, and if you weren't talking about Allah, then Annie wasn't listening.

---

Think outside of the box. Throwing bricks at the penitentiary has to stop. Out of envy and animosity, no one wants to see the next man on top. This unnecessary black-on-black crime has to stop.

We're losing all of our males to the system, the graveyard, and the streets. My brothers from different mothers, there's a million and one ways to eat.

One can control one's own destination through knowledge and education. Statistics say every African-American between the ages of 18 to 21 is, or has been, on parole, probation, or incarcerated.

Now take heed as I continue to fulfill my obligation. The Lord showed me mercy, so I can warn the people concerning temptation. The wicked can't run the race, there will be an elimination.

The righteous are on a mission to warn, save, and assist; it is their purpose. Yes sir, our God is giving us the occupation.

God is good all the time. God didn't abandon me or ever played tricks with my mind. The two set of footprints in the sand, when the other one disappears, God was carrying me, because I was weak. Please take heed to what I am saying…

By: Tray Austin

# CHAPTER 18

Zeek Bey got off the bus at the Greyhound Station in downtown Memphis. He decided to walk home since he lived roughly three miles away. He was accustomed to walking the prison track for one hour, which totaled twelve laps and equaled three miles, so today, Zeek Bey would get his exercise and sight-seeing.

While walking downtown past the Fed-Ex Forum, Zeek Bey ended up on Beale Street in Alfred's Bar and Grill. He counted his blessings to have a fresh start; as Zeek Bey walked further through downtown, he ended up on Poplar Street, and smiled upon seeing the Thunderdome, their infamous *201* County Jail. Zeek Bey thought about the time that one of his cellies said, *People in prison are low-lifers.*

Zeek Bey was fully aware that the guy was just speaking his opinion and had a lot to learn. So he voiced his belief, "People in prison are not low-lifers, they are just individuals who had to go through their low points in life to arrive at their blessings in life. We have all had to go through our seasons of growth. Low is the man that allows his fellow man to fall to the bottom without catching him in his fall. But in going through our lowest point, there awaits our blessings."

"Oh," was all the guy could say.

As Zeek Bey was going past Dixie Holmes projects, he saw a group of youngsters surrounding a skinny youngster. They pushed and shoved the young boy back and forth and took his eye-glasses. Their intention was to assault him verbally and to scare him until Zeek Bey arrived.

"It takes six of y'all for one man?" Zeek Bey asked.

"If you don't get on down that road, it's gonna be six

of us on YOU," Twon said, speaking for the entire group.

Zeek Bey started walking in their direction, hoping they were bluffing.

"Fool, you must got a deathwish," Love said, because there was going to be no backing down from him nor his group.

"Come on, Come on, tough guy," Jospe said, as he continued to wave Zeek Bey down to him and his crew. "Come on, boy, and once you cross that line, ain't no turning back. We got some good for you, big boy."

Zeek Bey didn't speak one word, he just continued walking as if he was hypnotized. His mind was blank, and he wasn't going to leave without the skinny kid.

The youngsters lit into Zeek Bey as if they were a nest of bees. They punched him. Zeek Bey didn't try to throw a punch, nor did he have a chance to. The youngsters beat Zeek Bey three quarters to death. Both eyes were swollen and bloody; his lips were busted, they'd kicked out four of his front teeth, his nose and ears were bleeding. Zeek Bey found strength from somewhere, because he began crawling to the skinny kid, who they had beat unconscious as well. Soon, Zeek Bey got close to the kid's body. One of the youngsters kicked him in the face, causing him to spread out on his back. The same youngster stood over Zeek Bey with his pistol aimed to Zeek Bey's chest. "Now, I'ma put a slug in ya chest." He pulled the trigger, shooting Zeek Bey in the shoulder instead of the chest, only because this was his very first time using the man-made killing machine.

Zeek Bey's body grew cold, and behind his eyelids, he revisited the time that him, Shakur, Sten X, Mr. Pete, and Baltimore Rick were playing chess, because during this moment of tragedy, these knowledgeable brothers brought him joy just by his being in their presence. This circle of wise guys was where he felt most comfortable, because he was amongst family.

A female screamed, “Someone call an ambulance! Somebody call an ambulance! A man and a little boy been beaten to death!”

“That's my neighbor's child!” identified the hood Big Momma. “She told her baby son to stop fooling around with that crowd of bad boys.”

“Soon as his mother turned her head, he'd sneak his tail right where they were at,” The hood's 2nd Big Momma in charge said. She was only second, because she was four years younger than Big Momma number one, but they both watched over their streets with equal care, trying to turn the young hoodlums into respectable young men, but always fighting a losing battle.

“He should have taken his mother's advice,” said the hood's Big Daddy.

He had all the respect in the hood, just like the Big Mommas did. When the youngsters were in his presence, no matter how bad a kid was, they didn't cuss or act up in front of Big Daddy, because they didn't want to disrespect him. Nobody was ever going to go against the Big Mommas or Big Daddy, because to go against them, was to go against the whole hood. Those three were always the first ones to the scene of a tragedy, always helping and police-ing their hood, giving advice, running the bad youngsters off when they were trying to get into trouble. They loved their Hood and tried to make it a better place.

“Did someone call the ambulance?” the female asked again, because everyone wanted to crowd and huddle amongst the scene.

“Yes.”

“They said they're on the way.”

Hood Big Momma number one advised that, wet

towels be placed on Zeek Bey and the small child's face and upper body. The crowd followed her instructions, until one woman decided she wanted to take charge and apply a towel with ice in it to Zeek Bey and the child's face.

"No Ice, chillins, no ice."

"Why?"

"Because I said so."

"Do as she say," the hood's Big Daddy coached.

The two elder ladies moved closer to Zeek Bey and the child's unconscious bodies. "I wonder what them old bats gonna do?" a youngster whispered.

"We gonna do what the wise do," one of the elder ladies said.

"And what is that?"

"Pray," Big Momma number two said, but Big Momma number one said, "We're gonna call the doctor!"

"Ain't no doctor around here! What doctor y'all crazy ladies talkin' bout?"

"Jesus. Jesus is our doctor," Big Momma number one stated, and she began humming, and then migrated into singing, and did not stop until both bodies were in the ambulance.

## GANGSTA, GANGSTA, GANGSTA, READ ALL ABOUT IT!!

# CHAPTER 19

Chase was led into the Federal Courthouse. Three Federal Marshals led the way, while five others walked beside him and behind him. They truly had Chase boxed in, so if he tried the slightest move, they'd be a couple of steps ahead of him. One of the Marshals kept his right hand on his belt holster. He hoped and prayed that Chase would try one wrong move, so he could splatter Chase's brains all over the courthouse walls. He and Chase had locked eyes several times, briefly. Every time Chase would look around sightseeing, he would always make eye contact with this same Marshal. Chase's first mind told him for the second and third time that the Marshals wanted him to try to escape, so he could play the hero.

"Keep going straight ahead," he said, giving Chase an order, which wasn't necessary, because one of the leading Marshals had previously announced they'd take the elevator, which plain as day was straight ahead, about fifteen feet.

Upon reaching their destination, one of the first three Marshals pushed the button to the elevator. As the lights were working their way down each button, he was tapping his right foot, as if he had some kind of nerve problem. Once the door opened, he walked into the back of the elevator and the other two Marshals followed, posting up on each side.

"You can go in now," another Marshal instructed.

Chase wasted no time completing the task. The first Marshal stayed staring straight ahead, so Chase did the same. Besides, he was afraid to try to turn around or to make any kind of movement without someone commanding him to do so. He did not want or need any kind of trouble or misconception with these guys, especially the one that was eyeballing him.

"Gum, gum anybody?" The Marshal that was eyeballing Chase offered.

"Sure, Bill, I could use a piece."

"No thank you, Bill."

"Billy boy, peppermint would have been better."

"Thanks, but I've got my own."

Chase heard the Marshal he was standing behind, and two others decline. As before, the same Marshal was tapping his foot again until the elevator opened, and to Chase's surprise, it opened facing him.

*That's why he didn't turn around*, Chase thought to himself, as he began to follow the leader slowly. He tried to walk, so the shackles around his wrists and ankles wouldn't cut into his skin as little as possible.

"We'll take a left up ahead," the leader announced.

Common sense told Chase that that sentence was for his ears only, because only God knows how many times these guys had matched and escorted people down this same hall and into the courtroom.

Once they made the turn, the courtroom's wooden double doors were straight ahead. "Three in and four out," the leader publicized, which he was accustomed to saying, and like always, he'll have the same three inside the courtroom, and the same four on the outside. The Marshals that guarded the double doors would take advantage of the free time and use it as their personal use by texting, paying bills with their phones, checking their e-mails. Occasionally, they'd play video games on their phones.

The courtroom was crowded, but not too crowded. There were more suits and ties along with other law enforcement officers than anything. The Marshals escorted Chase to his lawyer. They had to stand earshot away for eight to twelve minutes, due to the prosecutor needing to give Chase's lawyer a better understanding, because he did not have the time nor day for miscommunication, and he could care less if Chase was comfortable enough or not, because it wasn't his problem. He wasn't going to lose one good night's rest concerning this case.

"Yes"

"Yes."

"Yes."

"I understand."

"I agree."

It was no secret that Chase's public defending lawyer was a yes man, not to mention the fact that he and the prosecutor were golf partners as well as members of the same club. Their closets were full of skeletons, just as sure as grits are groceries.

As the prosecutor was making his entrance, the leading Marshal started moving forward. He extended his right hand to Chase's lawyer, "Hello, Ralf. How's everything coming?"

"Another day," Chase's lawyer said, as he accepted the outstretched hand and gave the Marshal a firm handshake. "Skip, you should try my job."

"No thanks, Pale."

"I know, I know. You've explained to me a million times, you just like to escort the prisoner, drop them back off, and high tail it back off," Chase's lawyer said with a smile.

"You got it, Pale."

"You've told me a million times."

"Well now," the Marshal paused long enough to steal a glance over in the prosecutor's direction, "Ain't you glad that we wouldn't have to make it a million and one."

Chase's lawyer was ready to do away with the small talk, because he was ready to wrap up this unfinished business. The sooner he could get his client free of the Marshal's hostage, the sooner he could get back to business elsewhere.

"Skip, you can take the shackles off of his wrists now," he addressed the lead Marshal.

"There'll be no need for the magic word this time," the Marshal replied, indicating the lawyer did not have to say please.

"Skip, thank you, you're the greatest."

"I know," the leader laughed out loud, "That's why I'm the expensive babysitter, and guess who's not?"

Chase's lawyer did not respond to that frivolous comment. It truly did not entertain his train of thought, because there laid a more important task that he needed to dismiss from his *Top Priority* list. Ralf took Chase by the elbow and carefully led him behind the two-seating wooden table; then he politely removed a couple of papers from his briefcase.

"You remember what we talked about?" the lawyer asked.

Chase played crazy. "We talked about a lot of things."

"The plea," the lawyer refreshed Chase's memory, and he did not hesitate.

"The plea bargain," Chase whispered out.

"It's in your best interest."

Chase swallowed, and I do mean hard.

"Take the plea," the lawyer advised, as he pushed the papers towards Chase. Chase gave the lawyer a crazy look.

"I even talked the prosecutor down from 30 years to 25 years."

"A whole quarter?"

"You go to trial, you get a life sentence."

"A quarter is a long ass time, ya heard me?"

"You murdered the guy!"

"How do you know? How can you say that?"

"We both know you did it," the lawyer said, as he toyed with the papers he needed Chase to sign.

"Who's side are you on?" Chase asked, with venom in his voice.

"If you continue to play around, you're going to wish you would have taken this plea, because the prosecutor might even take that life sentence off of the table and push for the death penalty."

"Can they do that?"

"The courts can do as they please."

While Chase was pondering and procrastinating, the element of surprise swung into action.

---

No matter what one does in the darkness, it shall be brought into the light. And one can be rest assured that someone will see something. Before Chase could get the blood off of his hands or the bloody clothes off his body, Sprinkler had called the agent and clearly stated that he'd just witnessed the murder, and he saw who killed Tray-L at U.S.P Petty Rock. Sprinkler didn't get the opportunity to work his life sentence off from the streets, nor was he fortunate enough to jump on people's cases that he was in prison with. He just so happened to be in the right place at the right time. Sprinkler was waiting on his supplier to bring him a spit-a-rette, but the guy failed to mention that he'd just gotten the coke bottle out of the trash that the officer had been spitting in all day. The guy had to pour the spit into his bowl, and dry the spit out in the microwave for about five minutes, before the dip converted back to smokable tobacco. The guy had to spoon feed the tobacco with the spit constantly, so the tobacco wouldn't dry too fast, plus the spit made the tobacco much stronger. Some guys favored spit-a-rettes over the real tobacco. They claimed it was stronger, but the truth being told, the spit-a-rette was a lot less expensive, and they would get more for their money. Yes, the quantity and the quality.

The transport agent led Sprinkler into the courtroom. He wore the same prison shackles as Chase. Sprinkler looked around for Chase, because he hadn't seen Chase since the murder took place. He spotted Chase sitting beside his lawyer. To Sprinkle, Chase's mind was on another planet, or he was discombobulated.

"Can we go up front?" Sprinkler asked the agent. He wanted to sit across from Chase or as close as he could to Chase.

"No."

Sprinkler wanted to ask why not, but decided not to.

"We don't need to move forward, until the prosecutor asks for you," the agent said, trying to put Sprinklers mouth and mind to rest.

Sprinkler just knew his testimony was going to get him a sentence reduction and that he'd be able to go to the F.C.I., so he wouldn't have to worry about all the tension in the air and politicians. No more shot-calling, because he was fed up with guys in his car telling him what he can and can't do. Putting his life and freedom on the line, because of something stupid that he did not do and made the situation his concern, behind someone from his state.

While Sprinkler's mind was occupied, Killer's agent escorted him, clean past him, and kept on trucking, until they were directly across from Chase and his lawyer. "Say Round, what's poppin'? Ya heard me?" Killer said, as he displayed a weak smile while being seated across the aisle from Chase.

Chase's face lit up like a Christmas tree. “Round, what are you doing here?”

“I came to man the fuck up. Woady, I'm a real nigga. I can't sit back and let these people take ya life for my shit. You took my first case; I'll be damned if I allow ya to take this one. Beside, Round, a nigga couldn't sleep at night.”

Chase's lawyer was looking from one mouth to the other, because he half understood them in their slang.

“Justin, what is this guy talking about?” the lawyer asked.

“That's my body, ya heard me? Lil one did not kill that piece of shit. That was my work.”

Killer's escorting agent handed over the papers that Killer had signed the same day he went into the Warden's office, and came clean. He demonstrated how he actually was stabbing Tray-L. The first knife punch was in the stomach, and he twisted the knife. The second blow was to the right side, with another strong repeat. And the last and final blow he hammered home, driving the twelve inch long, razor-sharp knife into the center of Tray-L's chest, making absolutely sure that his Christmas and New Year was canceled. If the knife wasn't laced with the braided sheet rope, the weapon would have slipped from his hand. Killer knocked so much blood out of Tray-L's body, that it was impossible for him to remain among the land of the living.

When Chase arrived, the damage was done. Killer pushed him back out of the room. Tray-L's blood and Killer's handprints were on Chase's shirt and wrists. Killer raced from the crime scene. Chase stood there for a few more seconds before he raced off, too.

Sprinkler was not the only one that saw this whole scene, other guys just chose to mind their own business. The guy that saw him destroying the murder weapon for

Killer had already sold Killer out, by immediately giving the captain the knife. Killer came forward and confessed, because his conscious was eating him. Plus, Playa gave him a heads-up warning that *Inmate.com* said there were at least five guys going to testify against him, and they weren't going to allow Chase to sell his soul to the belly of the beast.

The doctor advised Killer two weeks before, if he did not stop drinking liquor, smoking weed, and start back by taking his medication faithfully, that his liver cancer would take his very last breath away, before he reached one more birthday. The doctor couldn't have saved that breath, because it was like he was speaking Russian language, and Killer was speaking Chinese. His advice and instructions went in one of Killer's ears and out of the other one. The same night, Killer partied like a rock star. He increased all the *Don't Do's*. The next day, Killer spit up a couple of gallons of blood, and all that he didn't spit up, he threw up. As of today, his body felt tired; he had no energy. Killer wanted to get this over as soon as possible, so he could return to his deathbed. Seven more days surely wasn't in his favor.

"Round, I love ya, ya heard me?" Killer's weak voice echoed.

"I love you too," Chase replied.

The prosecutor rushed over to Chase and his lawyer. Chase began tearing up the plea papers. He never did sign his name on the dotted line.

"Mr. Prosecutor, I have a powerful God. He fought this battle for me."

"Ralf, I'm sorry. I apologize," the prosecutor said to Chase's lawyer.

"That was the Lord's work," Ralf stated to the prosecutor, then he turned to Chase. "Young man, always remember that it's never too late, and lots of people don't get a second chance. God has a reason for you being a free man. I don't know that reason. You'll have to take it up with God yourself. You young people always say that no one loves you... Justin, God loves you, and if you seek God's wise counsel, you will be a very, very wise young man.

"Am I free?" Chase asked.

"As a bird," the lawyer said.

"Round, my bad," Killer apologized, "For taking so long to step up to the plate, ya heard me?"

"Young man, you have a testimony the people definitely need to hear about," the lawyer said to Chase, as he patted him on the shoulder.

---

Officer Delta was taking the shackles off Chase's legs, so he could walk up the steps to his cell. The officer would always small talk with the prisoners, just to see where their head was. He's good for asking a couple dozen questions, nothing less than a dozen. The officer's first question popped off, "So, Justin, how are you today?"

"Blessed by the best and highly favored," Chase spoke these words into existence, and they would always roll off of his tongue without the smallest hesitation.

"God is good," the officer stated, trying to show Chase that he was versatile and could hold a conversation concerning any and every subject.

"God is a merciful God. If God is before you, who can be against you? God plays all positions."

"True, true, true," the officer said, being sarcastic. "I'll say amen to that!" The officer knew Chase's situation. Chase was facing the electric chair if the killer and the snitch wouldn't come forth. Chase would be heading to death row, instead of waiting for another couple of hours, before he'd once again be a free man.

"What you gonna do when you get out of jail?" the officer sang. "I'ma have me some fun!"

"Not me, I'm going to share my testimony and let the youngsters know that they truly don't want nothing to do with prison. Prison is the real bad man's land."

"I take it that you capitalize from your mistake?"

Chase cleared his throat and replied, "Children make mistakes. Grown people make bad decisions."

"Okay, okay," the officer nodded and continued his pimp walk, as he escorted Chase. "Justin, you said a mouth full."

"CO man, what I say good comes from God. And what I say bad comes from me."

Chase asked himself for the billion and one time, "Why didn't I have all this sense until when I was free? I used to say foolish stuff like God didn't love me, and if he did, why'd he allow me to get locked up? But I locked myself up by doing everything under the sun and moon that was totally against God's will. I was hollering about how God didn't love me, I couldn't have loved myself, because if I did, I wouldn't have been into everything but a casket. God allowed me to come here, so that I'll learn to love myself, and then I'll be able to love him. And God tells me that once we're able to love him, then we'll be able to have love for the people. I was a fake gangster, because I was afraid to get out of my element. Afraid to try something different... trying something different, now that's gangster. Stop following and become a man, cause men act off of their own intuition and emotion. Now there's a must that we elevate and educate. The world don't need anymore gangsters...cause there's a serious shortage of mentors and big brothers."

Define RELIGION:

The Unity in all religions is the fact that all of them speak of a creator ABOVE them.

The works they've done, you have the power to do greater EVOLUTION ......

# CHAPTER 20

Brother Darryll X Holmes and Brother Omar put together a beautiful Saviour's Day Program. They both would be the host, but brother Darryll rocked the mic first. "In the name of Allah, the Beneficent, the Merciful. As-salaam Alaikum." he greeted.

"Wa'alaikum-as-salaam," the chapel crowd greeted back.

"Peace be unto you," Brother Darryll X said the greeting again in English, since he'd used the Arabic language the first time.

"One God."

"One Goal."

"One Aim."

Brother Darryll X continued as he palmed the pulpit with both palms. "We need a foundation we can stand on! Days of division are over with! Happy Saviour's Day. We have to help one another... *Work Call* you heard! Now it's time we save ourselves. Our community needs you, needs us. The brothers that will speak today are here, because we love you. We have to uplift ourselves. It's time we study together. I need you. It's time we put our graphic location aside."

"Work Call!" Brother Omar's voice echoed.

"Nation building time," Darryll X Continued, "Whatever title you have, let's put that over to the side. I come with love and leave you with peace!"

Brother Omar strolled behind the pulpit smiling. He licked his lips, and he began to collect his thoughts. "Work Out!" he shouted.

"Work Call!" the crowd shouted back.

Brother Omar was days away from being back in

society. He was going to give the compound his last Khutbah for this Friday's Jumah, and the chapel was guaranteed to be packed, Insha-Allah, meaning If It's Allah's Will, because they enjoyed Brother Omar's message.

"Work Call!" Brother Omar shouted once more.

"Work Call!" they returned again.

"As-Salaam Alaikum," Brother Omar greeted.

"Wa'laikum-As-Salaam," the people greeted back.

Brother Omar studied the people's seating arrangement. The majority of the people were sitting in the last few back rows, and there were lots of unoccupied seats towards the front. "Brothers, move to the front, we've been sitting in the back of the bus for too long." He didn't feel comfortable within himself, if he didn't address this issue.

They took heed and got into compliance. Brother Omar finished sharing the knowledge, "Allahu-ala means Allah knows what's best. Brothers, Allah is the best of planners. All praises be to Allah, that we all are here today. Family, always allow your faith to move you, please by the gracious mind of Allah. Don't use your religious time out for separation, or time out for games. When you think like a champion, you will be a champion. When I think like a man, I will act like a man. Brush off limited thinking. The lord came and awakened you and I, the brothers in peace by the grace of Allah. Brothers, time and pressure will produce a beautiful diamond, and that's what Allah allowed us knowledgeable brothers to become, as a reward out of a prison term. Listen, when the brother first invited me to a Nation of Islam service, that was the best thing Allah and the brother could have given me. And family, it is important to me that every one of you brothers know I can't allow my religion to separate me from my brothers, my Christian brothers, and surely not my Sunni brothers."

He looked Shakur into the eyes, and Shakur nodded. Brother Omar nodded back and continued, "Family, y'all are locked up like me. I was the bad guy too, but I thank Allah that I am not the man who I used to be. We all have flaws. Family, we have to take to Allah, and to Allah's word and way of life, like a fish to a hook, and run with it. Family, by Allah allowing us to wake up every morning and to be in our right frame of mind, is a blessing. We have to stop taking the smallest things for granted. Now family, I'll come to a close here, because we need to take heed to what my brothers and your brothers have to say. Peace and blessing be upon all of you."

"Peace and blessings be upon you too, Brother Omar," they returned.

Brother Omar looked towards Shakur to see who would be the first guest speaker, so he could introduce him to the crowd, and the crowd surely had a lust for knowledge. "Beloved, you go first," Shakur addressed Rico, "and I'll go last," he continued, making it go without question that Sten X would be second as always. Young Rico began making his way to the pulpit. Brother Omar's voice did not hesitate to make the announcement immediately.

"Family, would you all give our beloved Brother Rico a round of applause for doing his duty, which surely, he could have neglected. May God be pleased with you, brother." Brother Omar said, giving Young Rico a firm handshake and a brotherly hug. Once Rico was behind the pulpit, he greeted them with the five letter word, Peace."

Everyone in the chapel shouted, "Peace!" out of love and respect. Young Rico's conscious began to unfold, as his two lips parted and his tongue began to rumble.

"Fear misunderstood is misused life. Fear: *False Evidence Appearing Real*. Fear is misapplied knowledge. Misapplied knowledge is the trait that captures not only the mind of man but the body as well."

"The human body produces a chemical called Endorphins. With this hyper compound, the brain goes into overdrive. One becomes narrow sighted as well as narrow-minded. To escape, one must broaden his horizon. We as a people confine ourselves to limited dreams. Thus crushing our own self-worth when they seem unattainable. Man must feel of substance, or he feels unworthy. To feel worthy, one must work. Work to educate self and surrounding. Slaughter is easy when there is no unity. To unite, one must conquer the false teachings and be brave enough to be different. Allow your bright light to shine!"

"Some of you, I believe, got the message. A lot of you, I challenge to be honest with yourselves, because you are the epitome of what I just spoke on. Instead of getting a clear understanding of what I just spoke on, you agreed, because of how you would look being different. This is the foolish pride of man, his EGO. This is the poison we place into our communities, misunderstood or flawed knowledge. This cancerous information destroys from the inside. Wrong information can have negative consequences. It misguides people and closes the spectrum of thoughts and dreams. They place limitations on a limitless life. So brothers, I encourage you to be standup men and not be ashamed to say *I don't know,* or break it down, or please elaborate. This is GROWTH. Growth is a verb. It's a continuous action. Life is action. Growth and death are synonymous, they both deal with the completion's end. There is no more action. Please start with your own vocabulary and get rid of the words with negative effects and impressions."

"Then take what you have, mold it, and teach your surroundings. This is the way to make an impact on a society that counts you as inferior, for them to see the truth of our evolution and growth as individuals and as a people."

"With these basic principals, we start breeding soldiers. Soldiers are bred, not born. We've made that error of putting big expectations on small minded people. The individuals were not bred for the positions, nor were they adapt to sustain a level of consciousness, because they lived an adverse life and were never taught. Stop allowing time and experience to teach. Our trials and tribulations should not be repeated by our offspring. Educate them well before the experience take place, for it to be avoided. Contrary to popular belief, the Game is to be told."

When Young Rico finished, Brother Darryll X returned behind the pulpit and said, "y'all please give that young knowledgeable brother another big round of applause. And I thank Allah for the brother coming out today to share his knowledge with you and I." Darryll briefly paused, acknowledging Shakur to see who would be the next speaker, but common sense told Sten X, that was his cue. Sten X began wheeling his way to the pulpit.

"Brothers, would you all be kind enough to give my brother and your brother, Sten X a round of app1ause."

Brother Darryll X and Sten X exchanged Salaams and after their religious style of brotherly hug, Sten X parked his wheelchair beside the pulpit and began to drop it like its hot. He was ready to give the people the 411.

"In the name of Allah, the Beneficent, the Merciful... we give him praise and thanks for his mercy and his goodness to the human family, that whenever we stray from the path of righteousness, that Allah always raises up one from among the people, to guide them back to his straight path. So we thank HIM for Moses, or Musa, and the Torah, we thank him for Jesus, or Isa, and the gospel. We thank him for Muhammad Ibn Abdullah and the revelation of the Holy Qur'an. Peace be upon these worthy servants of Allah. I am a student of the Teachings of the Most Honorable, Elijah Muhammad... I can never thank Allah enough for his intervention in our affairs. I bear witness that there is no God but Allah, who appeared to us in the form of Master Fard Muhammad, to whom praises are due forever, and raising one up from among us, the black man, here in the wilderness of North America ...to be a divine leader, teacher, and guide, in The Most Honorable Elijah Muhammad. And if I live to be a thousand years old, I could never thank Allah enough, for leaving in our midst a divine reminder, living example and standard-bearer, in the Honorable Minister, Louis Farrakhan. It is in these three men's name that I greet you all in the Nation's greeting words of Peace and Paradise, and we say it in the Arabic language ...As-Salaam Alaikum."

"Dear Family, welcome to Saviour's Day."

"This day, Saviour's Day, was established by the Most Honorable Elijah Muhammad, to commemorate our savior, Master Fard Muhammad, who blessed us with a driving knowledge of self, knowledge of God, and our open enemy, the devil. It was within this body of Divine Knowledge that the Most Honorable Elijah Muhammad taught us that the Blackman was, and is in fact, the Original Man ...the Maker, the Owner, the Cream of the Planet Earth, God of the Universe."

"Typically, I would teach on this man ...Fard Muhammad, his student, and messenger Elijah. However, most of the basic information is on the program and additional handout that was on your seats. I believe the best way to open up this program is to first have a moment of silence ...for our ancestors, those male and female warrior, who have given their lives for the liberation and upliftment of our people. A moment of silence for the many lives that are taken daily by the enemy, who continues to show us he does not give a damn about us.

For the lives of our babies, our young sons, and daughters ..."

Sten held up a copy of The Final Call Newspaper, with the front page caption, HAVE YOU HAD ENOUGH? He asked the audience, "Have YOU had enough?"

"YES!," the audience replied together.

"Before I go forward, I want to thank Dread for the Black History Program he sponsored, entitled *Moving Forward*, where it was questioned whether black history is relevant. As long as we have an open enemy who continues to whitewash and hide our greatness as a people from us ...an enemy who wishes to begin the so-called American Negro's history with slavery, an enemy who continues to define who we are, what we are, and puts limitations on what we can do, yes, we must have Black History. We must immediately stop allowing the enemy to tell us our history. Any time your enemy gives you a historical background on yourself, you can best believe it will always paint him in the best picture. His version of our history keeps us divided, so I see no connection to my brothers in Central and South America, the Caribbean, or even on the continent of Africa. Allah (SWA) teaches us in the Holy Qur'an 49:13 that from a male and female, he made us tribes and families, that we may know each other. In this chapel today, we have many tribes. Many groups, many different religions, brothers from everywhere. Nevertheless, these differences should never be greater than our desire to be free people."

"I want to thank Brother Frank for putting together a Black History program, that dealt with Oneness and Blackness ... We are one! Or rather, we should be one. When a brother gets on the compound, we ask him where he's from... Once he tells us, if it's not where we're from, we direct him to his homeboys. But the Spanish and whites look out for their own, regardless of where they are from."

"Oneness...We must become one, despite our differences, if we are going to change our condition as people. We have to begin to love ourselves...The Honorable Elijah Muhammad taught those of us who follow his teachings, that we must love our people more than they hate themselves. Now that's a hell of a thing. That takes work, that takes dedication, and that takes sacrifice. We didn't call you out here today just to impress you with our talk, or make you think we've got it together. No, we are all students, and we struggle daily with these teachings, but the more practice we have, the more our lives change for the better. Prophet Muhammad (PBUH) taught us that, a Muslim is not a Muslim, until he wants for his brother what he wants for himself. We want you to have what we have ...It's like that fine weed. That Chronic, INDO, or whatever they call it. When you hit it, it has you feeling so good! So you call up your men. Well, we took a hit of these Teachings today...KUSH! Once you get some, you gotta smoke some with your man and say, Man, I got that fire...it's that fire ...What's up? Think about it, dear family, as I leave you with a quote from Farrakhan ...the cause for which we are gathered here today is bigger than all of us who are gathered, and therefore, it is incumbent upon us to submerge our personalities, even our different methodologies, religious persuasions, or the lack thereof, for the cause that is bigger than us all ...The Unification of our people! Welcome again to Savior's Day! How Strong is our Foundation? Can we survive? I leave you as I came ...in peace! As-Salaam Alaikum!"

Brother Omar pimp-walked behind the public, smiling, displaying his gold front teeth. "My brother Sten X got that fire, huh? Brother Young Rico got that fire, huh? Now, family, put y'alls hands together to give our big brother, Shakur, a warm welcome. This beautiful brother is truly, a soldier for Allah. He's our peacemaker."

As Shakur exchanged greetings with Brother Omar, he kept account In-Sha-Allah meaning, If it's the will of Allah, that this too would be his last group speaking. So he decided to elaborate on Young Rico and Sten X's issues as well as some of his own, so the guys would have the best of three worlds. Shakur smiled at Young Rico, because he liked how he spoon fed the people. *May Allah be pleased with Young Rico. Insha-Allah, he'll continue sharing the knowledge with the people. May Allah continue blessing and increasing him with knowledge*, Shakur thought to himself. Then he decided not to keep the people waiting any longer.

"The use of guns to vent our frustration and express our anger on those who look like us, to feel tough and masculine based on a distorted sense of manhood, only to take away lives needed in the fight to save ourselves and add more casualties to the war we are already losing. Drug dealing, drug abuse, and guns used for black-on-black violence are taking away our best and our brightest. These two elements, guns, and drugs, are the primary basis of our crime in our communities. And by these two, our people are packed in prisons by their hundreds of thousands."

"The ultimate enemy is ignorance, and our adversaries have used our ignorance as a tool to subjugate us. If the impoverished masses would truly realize that poverty is a state of mind first and foremost, and if we would recognize that collectively, we possess an abundance of wealth if we would combine and utilize the resources we have at our disposal. We could really change the state of our existence and rid our communities of ills, such as poverty and crime."

"We must understand that the essence of economics is based on the cooperation of proportions to the principal of the central structure thus, it is the mutual interaction and exchange of resources and finances, adhering to the primary function of cooperation, in order to generate wealth and keep it circulated, so that the principal structure can be maintained. So, in essence, the very life of economics is a community endeavor. And likewise, poverty is the consequence of economic dis-cooperation and aversion to the principle of harmony and cooperation - the fragmentation of the central structure into isolated units, that restrict the flow and circulation of the general source, creating disparity and barriers to the function of other proportions. In layman's terms, men hoarding bread from their fellow man."

"Fragmented, economic monopolization is a crime- in truth, the ultimate crime, because it systematically deprives people of the right to forward mobility, in effect, causing the condition that makes poverty, which in turn gives birth to crime."

"I'll say it again; crime is the ill-conceived child of poverty and ignorance, which is the ill effects of institutionalized racism and systematic oppression. When you have destitute people living in impoverished conditions, without any knowledge of the process it takes to free themselves from such circumstances, blind and desperate, lacking basic necessities, and faced with the dilemma of daily survival, you have laid the foundation for crime and all the other deplorable acts that occur. Just ask the cat in federal prison serving a thirty-year sentence for a few ounces of crack cocaine, and he'll tell you, *If feeding myself is a crime, then I am guilty as charged."*

"I greet you brothers in the ancient Kemetic (Egyptian) greeting of peace, all peace. May blessings and strength be upon you all. With that said, I humbly ask that you brothers, lend me your ear for the time being. I would like to convey a message of encouragement from my heart to yours."

"My dear brothers, up until now, we have been lost,

confused, misguided, scared, unstable, and self-destructive, trapped in the abyss of darkness and ignorance, groveling on our knees, blind without a sense of direction, and existing as hopeless slaves to deplorable circumstances."

"I say up until now, because now is the dawn of a new day. Now, means right here, where we stand. Now is the present moment, it is not confined to the context of time. It has no recollection of prior events; it manifests itself in this very instant, it is the only true reality. The past is just that - the past. The future remains to be seen and for now, it is only a distant vision. Its ultimate outcome will be determined by what we do now. So, let go of the past, because it has no bearing on right now - only if you allow it. And do not be too preoccupied with the future without being firmly grounded in the present, because if you do, you will only be infatuated with a dream and lost in an illusion."

"I say up until now, because now is the time to embrace the very best of yourself, to forgive yourself for your mistakes and failures, and take the oath to achieve your manhood and establish the divine within you, as the central and guiding force in your life. Right now, not tomorrow, not in few weeks, but now, and not a day late. You have the power within you to rectify yourself and transform your situation from one of conflict and strive to peace and prosperity. You have only been wretched because you have thought in that manner. You have only been fearful and discouraged, because you have abided by the dictates of your weaker state."

"But now, that is no more. Now, your consciousness has awakened. Your soul has risen from its slumber, and the divine essence of your being, is proclaiming to you, I am that I am. I am power. I am might. I am a ruler. I am a master."

"Right now, you can decide the path that you will

walk from here on out. All you have to do is turn within and consult your own heart, and you will hear that quiet, still voice say with all certainty, that now is the time. Go on and claim your glory and declare your greatness. Don't be afraid. Fear has left you now. You are no longer a weak being intimidated by the challenges of life, you are the master of yourself, and you rule strong and reign supreme within the kingdom of your existence."

"Now is the time to crown your mind with enlightenment and sit upon the throne of virtue. Take your place. Today, you are king, master, and ruler. And you will prosper and be victorious…here, now, and forevermore."

"In closing, pray that Allah gives us eyes to see, ears to hear, a mouth to speak truthfully, a mind to think wisely and correctly, feet to walk the righteous path, hands to do good deeds, and a pure and clean heart, so that we may serve ourselves and humanity with love and compassion. I leave you brothers in the same way I came ...peace, all peace."

Brother Darryll X got back behind the pulpit and politely asked the people to give Shakur and the other speakers a round of applause. Then he left the floor open for anyone who wanted to speak. Big Buck stood and said he'd like for everyone to close their eyes and bow their heads, so he could thank the Lord as well for allowing this event to take place. Big Buck's young homies called him Uncle Buck, out of respect.

Big Buck began delivering his message by his seat, because walking to the pulpit would have been too much work.

"Our Father, who art in Heaven, hallowed be thy name. Thy Kingdom come, thy will be done, on Earth as it is in heaven. Give us this day our daily bread, and forgive us our trespasses, as we forgive those who trespass against us. And lead us not into temptation, but deliver us from evil. For thine is the kingdom, and the power, and the glory forever. Amen..."

Once Big Buck finished, Brother Omar hollered "Work Call!"

And the people repeated, "Work Call!"

"Now, family, since we all know it's our duty to awaken the people, I look forwawrd to everyone trying to live up to the expectation of being one of the chosen ones."

"Insha-Allah," someone whispered.

"Allahu-Ala," Shakur mumbled.

---

They made me the villain and hide me from society,
I was changed 100 to 1 for only a quarter key.
I was sentenced, 27 years into the federal
penitentiary. When I got in my 40's, I came to reality.
My heavenly father, Allah provided and protected
me, Got me like the blind man once said, now I can see.
Who want for my past to be their future? The insane
things I and my character did only for TV.
I thank my precious and most merciful Lord, for
allowing me this blissful opportunity.
And deep down in my heart, I sincerely hope and
pray the forthcoming male generation, don't make as
many mistakes and very bad decisions as I did.
Please, don't allow the criminal way be your trials
and tribulations, nor served as your education, and
certainly not as your occupation.
I'm a living witness the feds wouldn't lose not one
good night of sleep, when they bury you alive in the
belly of the beast.
Everything good I say comes from the Lord; my

people avoid that run-in with the alpha boys.

Nothing can be done without the assistance of our powerful and merciful Lord.

You know why the horses wear those patches over their eyes, when they race around the track? So they will stay focus and stay on track.

I salute the nation.

# CHAPTER 21

"If you don't eat your apple, let me know, because they are very healthy for you. You don't have to sell them to me," Damage announced several times, as he paraded around in the unit. One day out of the week, the institution cooked on the grill; mostly on Wednesday's, but sometimes on Thursdays. The lunch would be passed out on a white styrofoam tray, in front of the kitchen. Damage was 40 years old and had the mentality of a sixteen-year-old. He would talk all day about nothing. He would talk and lie just because he had a mouth. The more knowledgeable one becomes, the less interest he/she would have, in common with certain individuals.

Damage had not been in prison for four days, and he was changing the TV, mingling with any and everybody, good and friendly. The people say that he's wild and knew he had a head with no screw, playing with half a deck, nutty as a fruitcake. Everyone knew that he didn't wrap to tight, soon as he opened his mouth. Conscious tried to bring something to Damage's attention, but Damage wanted to talk instead of listen. So now, Conscious doesn't talk to him period.

Last night, Damage was reading the Bible, while listening to Lil Boosie's music on the MP3 player. Conscious asked him how it was possible? Damage justified the strong lyrics was nothing but soft music to him. The next night, Damage stood on the top tier dancing with a loud orange, reddish hat on his head. Yes sir, Urkel #2. The third-night Damage just started talking out of the blue, hollering about he, being a real nigga! A solid nigga! Conscious asked him what the definition was of a real nigga?

"African American."

"What's the meaning of a solid nigga?"

"The same," Damage said, "an African American."

"You're wrong."

"What's the meaning of a nigga then?" Damage asked.

"An ignorant person," Conscious enlightened, "Any race or color can be a nigga." Damage was ignorant, and some. He was good and stupid.

"If a white guy called you a nigga, or said *what up my nigga*, you would be trying to kill him," Conscious said.

"No, I won't, cause I ain't never been a slave before."

"Bruh, please forgive me, I am sorry for getting in your lane," Conscious tried to excuse himself.

"A real nigga is the street language of street niggas. What we call solid niggas," Damage said. "Niggas here fuck with me, cause they know that I am a solid nigga."

Conscious frowned this conversation because it was irritating, "Bruh, you forty years old. You have to do away with the 'N' word and the nickname. It's time for you to bring out that grown man way of life. You have children?"

"Five."

Conscious knew this was somebody's father; there was nothing he could teach them. Damage admitted that he had been in and out of prison all his life, and this wasn't his first rodeo. His first bid he had done ten years straight, now he claimed that God sent him back this time, so that he could get his G.E.D. The man had been in the G.E.D. class longer than doctors went to school. Yes, he invested over fifteen years.

Conscious went to rec to avoid his celly, because engaging in conversation with Damage was a waste of time and energy. It is so sad, but so true, trying to drop jewels on Damage was surely casting your pears among the swine.

Sten X was the talk of the compound. His case manager gave him the legal mail, and it was from his lawyer, clearly stating that his case would be dismissed, and he could walk Scott free if he was willing to sign, stating he wouldn't try to sue the system for the illegal injustice. The lawyer and prosecutor immediately notified his unit team of their conference call with Sten X, 8 a.m sharp in the morning.

Conscious found Sten X riding the elliptical machine, which he would ride for 45 minutes to an hour, after walking one hour around the track. This was his five days; a week medication, what he prescribed for himself, to win his health back. Sten X truly didn't need the wheelchair anymore, but he continued to use the chair as a walker, as he strengthened his legs.

“Peace Brother?” Conscious greeted.

“Peace, bruh,” Sten X returned the greeting.

“I heard about the good news,” Conscious said smiling. He was very happy for Sten X, and personally thought it couldn’t have happened to a better person.

“Bruh, I needed that loophole,” Sten X confessed, a loophole is something illegal of what prisoners called injustice or a way out of prison. Or a way to get their sentences overturned, if not vacated.

“Congratulations.”

“Thanks.”

“So you outta here tomorrow?”

“I'll have the conference call in the morning,” Sten X said, as he fought to continue fighting the pain in his legs. “Once I sign the papers stating I wouldn't sue them concerning my case, I'm free, my case manager says he'll fax them the papers, and I should be free as a bird by noon.”

“Bruh, you should've told him you'll sign on the dotted

line now. Why put off tomorrow, what can be done today," Conscious said.

"Bruh, you know I did," Sten X managed to wolve out.

"You are working that machine as if you getting prepared to walk or run all the way home," Conscious said.

Sten X got off the machine and drained a bottle of lemon water, once he caught his breath, he said, "Bruh, your day coming, because God's still in the blessing business." Sten X told everyone the same line that congratulated him.

"Where Big Bro?"

"Shakur in the unit, he'll be back out next move. He had to call his cousin, because his cousin says that things are starting to look good in his case as well. And if things go according to plan, he also will be a free man," Sten X revealed.

"Insha-Allah."

"Insha-Allah," Sten X repeated Conscious saying, if its the will of Allah.

"Allah is a mysterious God."

"A merciful God."

The next day around lunchtime, everything worked out according to plan; Sten X was getting an immediate release. There were 1600 inmates on the compound, 900 which walked with Sten X, as Shakur and Conscious escorted him to the R&D. The staff had a misconception, that the mob was walking someone to the LT. office, running them off the compound, checking them in, until they recognized Shakur and knew that everything was peaceful. But out of fear of one of the staff, he hit the deuces, causing other staff to drop whatever they were doing and race to the chow hall.

"Everything is in compliance," the warden announced to all of his employees. "Douglas and his people walking Peabody to R&D to say their goodbyes."

"All the people?" a school teacher asked, because they did put the fear of God in her, since there was a beautiful demonstration.

"Peabody is an important man," another staff member said. "He is a likable guy," another C.O. stated.

"Peabody and Douglas keep down alot of the foolishness on the compound. They keep the peace," a LT publicized.

"They are soldiers for the Lord," another LT spoke, "I heard them both speak in the Chapel and on the yard plenty of times. They don't condole the BS."

The staff watched in disbelief, as the entire prison population shook hands with Sten X and gave him a brotherly hug. It was amazing of the power and influence that Sten X had with his brothers from different mothers.

"Brother Shakur, I know I'll see you on the other side real soon. Big Brother, Allah's going to bless you, as though he has blessed me," Sten X said, hoping to talk things into existence.

"Bruh, you be safe and stay on your square. Don't allow anything, nor no one to convert you back into the old you. I love you Brother."

"I love you too, Shakur."

"Sten X, that God work," one of the wise brothers hollered, as they all witnessed Sten X walk through the R&D doors.

After he finished dressing into the clothes that his mother sent him, he had to clear three checkpoints by stating his name and number proving that he was Peabody. Once he arrived to the last officer, she informed him that his father was waiting out front. Sten X never knew his father. His mother told him that his father got murdered when he was 12 years old. Sten told his mother, that she was his father and mother.

Big Ro stood by the back door of his latest model Bently; the female chauffer stood in front of the door, center of the vehicle. Sten X and Big Ro smiled upon seeing one another. Sten X walked in a slow pace, because he was still trying to become accustomed with walking without his wheelchair. He walked into Big Ro's embrace.

"Thank God you are a free man," Big Ro stated.

Sten X never heard Big Ro use such language. God never came into the equation. God has changed Big Ro's heart, Sten X thought.

"Its good to be free," Sten X confessed.

Once they were seated into the back of the car, the chauffeur closed their back door and got back into traffic.

"You hungry? Where would you like to eat?"

"I am good, maybe later."

Big Ro poured himself a drink. "You want a glass of wine?"

"No more devil, water for me."

Big Ro took small sips. "Son, I'm going to give you a million in cash. What are you going to do with all that money?"

"I will buy all the guns that money can buy," Sten X said, without giving the question much thought.

"Why?" Big Ro asked, before taking another sip of wine.

"Because I want to get as many guns off the streets as possible."

The chauffeur had to steal a glance in her rearview mirror, for she needed to look at Sten X, for what just came out of his mouth.

"Sten, why would you do something as dumb as that?" Big Ro asked, because that was something that he needed to hear.

"Because it will be pleasurable to Allah."

---

You offended me, I'll say you right, and I'm wrong
Like Rodney King said, can't we all just get along
By me being conscious, you'll say I'm deep
I'll reply by saying, you haven't been awaken, you're still asleep
There's millions and millions of ways to eat, to get on your feet
We were lazy thinkers, that's why we landed in the belly of the beast
Which forced me to wake up, smell the coffee, and count my blessings,
cause I could have easily been in a coffin
My wicked way, them unnecessary forbidden caves, and tragedy days was my ingredients,
Now, you know how I was made
Now, I scatter these seeds, asking the forthcoming generation to please take heed: Criminals, killers, and gangsters, our communities no longer need. Lawyers, doctors, and another Obama surely, indeed
God used my sinful body to try to share the knowledge with somebody, who wants to be somebody. God spared me for this occupation. God needed me, yes, the career criminal, to birth not one, but two parts of Trans-4-Mation.

# CHAPTER 22

Mr. Jay shaved his salt and pepper beard because he was trying to knock two years off his age. He wanted to be underneath that sixty-five mark. He was the people's champ. They loved to see him coming, because no-one could put a smile on their face like Mr. Jay. No matter what misery one might be in, the old head would put something on the mind, that would lighten the burden.

He taught how to kill two birds with one stone, by becoming Ms. Ab tutor and assisting the youngest with getting their GED. Since he was wise enough to know these present dudes can and will lie about being Superman. And it was their story, and they would stick to it. Mr. Jay heard so many of the youngest stories, about how they were living large and stacking money. They always talked about what interests them. So in his class, he issued them street novels, to get them to read more, which were several folds for the learning process. With knowledge, comes the ability to support one's self. Mr. Jay keeps them competing, challenging themselves and each other. Since they all were in the same boat, sink or swim. He allowed no-one to be criticized. Mr. Jay stated if any criticizing would take place, he would be the one and only to dish it out, and that would be private, in an one-on-one section. Mr. Jay's classroom board read, negative words would not be spoken in class, such as stupid, dumb, nor ignorant. Can't no-one put no-one down, always encouraging one another.

Mr. Jay preached, "The most you can even do, is the best you can. No-one can expect more of you, and you shouldn't expect anything less of yourself."

The Urban novels helped develop memories, word identification, word association, and memory compensation. They assists them to get more selected about what they read to build a good foundation and confidence. They elevated to a higher reading level and began reading Red Austin Novels.

Yes, sir. Mr. Jay assisted the guys to escape the elementary stuff; *The Worm and Frog,* first grader books. Easy through the fourth-grade level, while working on the sixth to eighth-grade level, some of the guys dropped out loosing eleven good days for not going to school.

Mr. Jay enjoyed talking to Damage, since he made the statement, he was a Muslim and a Christian. Mr. Jay asked him, why he eats Pork Skin.

"Because I ain't ate them in a long time," Damage said, "You didn't see me when I ate the pork sausages. I bet-cha? Because if you did, you would have said something."

"How do you pray?" Mr. Jay just had to ask.

"I ain't gotta answer that question, cause you ain't no Don," Damaged stated looking serious.

"Then can you tell me why you quit coming to G.E.D. class."

"I quit, cause they ain't teaching nothing."

"You sure ain't trying to learn nothing."

Mr. Jay already knew Damage was good and through, meaning not too bright. He always addressed Damage with, "there goes my friend that had the barbershop in the basement or in the backyard of his grandmother's house."

"Help me get my G.E.D, Mr.Jay?"

"Damage, I pulled your test scores, it'll take you years."

"I ain't stupid."

"I did not say that," Mr. Jay said, "I don't use such words."

Damage hunched up his shoulders, “I’m just saying.”
“Do you know all of your timetables?”
“Come on Mr. Jay.”
“Okay, start with your nines?”

Mr. Jay showed him how to do them on his fingers, because he wanted Damage and the other guys to have correct answers and to stop always guessing.

When the guys try to pull the wool over Mr. Jay eyes concerning they know this or that. He’ll have them to put a fireball into his jar for every wrong answer. It never fails, the guys who claimed to know it all, were the ones to fill the jar with fireballs.

“The dumbest question is the one never asked.”

---

I used to be an animal for that cheddar.
I'd let the sinful way go, stop working for the devil.
Trick him devil, trick him devil, trick him devil,
O my mighty lord, help the people, protect my people.
I was misled as Eve deceived Adam, I transformed into a paper-chaser,
Once I bit into the beautiful juicy apple.
The more money I got, I was blinded by my greed.
I hunted and hunted, even at times, that I did not need.
I was young and dumb, anything stupid, you could count me in, I wanted some, and I had an attitude like a ticking time bomb.
I always keep my eyes on the prize, by the devil I got hypnotized, but now all praises be to God, the Lord opened my eyes.
I had a one-way ticket, to the penitentiary or the graveside, before I reached the age of 25, the old

people's vision was so true, I was buried alive.
I was stuck in one foolish gear, the devil stayed and
played in my ear, Grandmomma stayed praying for me
and at my sentencing, like a baby, she cried.
I was not suicidal, but homicidal? Was I retarded? Was I
crazy?
Now it's gonna take the whole world to come
together to save these babies.

# CHAPTER 23

"Today, a fifteen-year-old male teenager was beaten half to death. Also, the other male victim was just released from prison. Witnesses say Zeek Wilson was walking past Dixie Holmes Projects, when he saw a gang beating the teenager, and he single handedly tried to fight off the mob. Both victims are in critical condition," the news reporter reported, as Zeek Bey and the teenager's faces were in the corner of the screen. Zeek became the talk of the town. Three days later, his co-defendant, Hammer, learned about the situation, and Hammer had a little power in the streets. When he asked questions, the streets answered back.

He went to visit Zeek, but he was still in a comma. Hammer informed the nurses, he was Zeek's brother and asked to be notified immediately, once he opened his eyes.

Behind Zeek Bey's eyelids, his memory was loaded with prison activities, prison projects.

He came out of his comma laughing and spitting out blood. The nurse rushed to his rescue providing him with aids and assistance. "Mr. Wilson, its good to have you back with us," she said, as he made sure he didn't choke on his own blood. She pushed him onto his back, until he was in a sitting position. Zeek Bey released a mouth full of blood into the blue plastic bowl.

"Its good to be back among the land of the living."

"Young man, you had internal bleeding, but it stopped now, praise God."

"How long have I been in here?"

"Five days and you've been in that nasty comma the whole time," she updated. "Oh, I almost forgot. Your brother was here. He told me to give him a call as soon as you opened your eyes."

"What brother?" Zeek Bey wanted to say, but decided to keep his trap shut and allow her to run off at the mouth, because he could learn a lot by listening.

Once she finished tending to Zeek Bey, the nurse kept her promise, by giving Hammer a phone call.

"Your brother woke up."

"Thank you, I am on my way."

Hammer walked into Zeek Bey's room shortly. He only lived a quarter mile away from the hospital. He was slim, grey by the head, and beard. Zeek Bey almost didn't recognize him.

"What's up, bro? How you feeling?" Hammer asked, while shaking his head.

"Hammer, why you so skinny and grey?" Zeek Bey asked, as he leaned forward, so the nice nurse could place the pillows in his back, so he could sit more comfortably.

"How is that, Mr. Wilson? Are you more comfortable?"

Zeek Bey wasn't accustomed to this kind of treatment. He felt special, extra special, because the place where he came from, the medical people would not do their J.O.B. They would get an attitude with the inmates and prison for seeking medical assistance.

"I am a man who counts all blessings, big or small," Zeek Bey said, smiling at the nurse.

"I will give ya'll young men some privacy," she said, exiting the room.

"Zeek, I would like to thank you for not taking me to jail with you," Hammer begin. "Bruh, that was some real nigga shit."

"Grown man shit," Zeek corrected. "I know that's not how you got grey in the face and head?" Zeek Bey joked.

"Bruh, my lifestyle got me grey and kept me stressed."

Now, that was something that Zeek Bey did not want

to discuss, nor encounter, so he immediately changed the discussion, before Hammer could elaborate and get deeper into detail.

"So how did you find me?"

"The news," Hammer stated. "Soon as they showed your picture and mentioned your name, I came straight here. As soon as the nurse told me you were in a comma, I knew it wouldn't do you any good for me to sit around here. So I went into the streets, where I could do you some good. I went out and ran them dudes down, who did this to you. You saved my ass, so that's what I've done for you. It is a start, on the way of showing my appreciation."

"You know all of them?"

"Every single one of them."

"Bruh, you got to be kidding me?" Zeek Bey said in disbelief.

"I lie to you not, brother," Hammer said, as he cut his eyes over to Young Kelo. "I brought the shooter with me." Hammer failed to mention, he and the shooter's mother had a good report back in the days. And that he needed this issue to be over with today, and everything to be swept under the rug.

Hammer explained to Young Kelo, that Zeek Bey wasn't the type to talk to the law, because if that was the case, he would have been arrested with Zeek Bey.

"He's the shooter? The one who shot me?" Zeek Bey asked, and wanted to ask Hammer how he got the youngster to come to the hospital, but abandoned the idea and decided to speak on the most important of issues.

"Lil bruh, you shot me?"

" Yes."

"Why?"

"Because at the time he thought, it was the right thing to do," Hammer spoke on Kelo's behalf. "The youngster days now is wild'n out, like me and you, used to be."

Zeek Bey understood and decided the past is the past,

because only the future is what counts. So he only wanted to speak on the future.

"Lil bruh, do you apologize for what you have done to me?"

"Yes sir."

"I need you to promise me that this type of unnecessary conduct won't occur again." Zeek Bey said, in a fatherly tone of voice. "I just got out of prison, and lil bruh, they got places to lock you up and throw away the key. The places I've been, you do not want to go to. The system plays for keeps. Daily, you are faced with life-threatening situations, where you have to take a life or lose your life in the process. You don't need that, and I don't want that for you. Those places are filled with bad guys. Always stabbing, killing, without any rules to fighting."

"A whole lot of killing?" Kelo asked, in his little boy voice.

"Too much unnecessary killing."

"Like on the streets?"

"Yes," Zeek Bey nodded, sadly.

"Kelo, it is time for you to change," Hammer stated, hoping that Kelo would take heed.

"There's a bigger picture," Zeek Bey said. "Life is beautiful, lil bruh. I did not know that life was so beautiful, until I got behind these walls. I allowed my life to slip through my fingertips."

"You're back here with us now."

"Yes," Zeek Bey smiled through his pains. "By the grace of God."

Zeek Bey talked and talked, until Hammer said that he had to get Kelo back, and he promised Zeek Bey, that he'd return before the day was over.

The skinny kid's mother waited patiently, so she could speak with Zeek Bey in private. As well as to thank him for trying to assist her son. Soon as young Kelo and Hammer exited the room, she asked the nurse to ask Zeek, if she could have a few minutes of his time.

"Sure, please send her in," Zeek Bey replied to the nurse.

Once Vakeita stepped into the room, the hospital room got too small for both of them. They were not too familiar with names, but they could not forget a face.

Zeek Bey had just gotten out of prison for carjacking her. They both went back down memory lane ...

*"Nice car," the bag boy said, as they walked up to her spotless burgundy LS400.*

*"Thanks." Vakeita smiled. She unlocked the trunk for the bag boy, as he placed the groceries in for her, she secured her son in the car seat. She handed the bag boy a handsome tip, thanking him for his service, as she sat down behind the wheel of her car. She was rummaging through her purse for a piece of candy, when she heard someone snatching on the door handle. Vakeita looked up at Zeek like he was crazy, not frightened the least.*

*"Okay bitch, you got the door locked, huh? Oh, I got something for that," Zeek gritted, pulling the pistol from under his shirt. He drew back and swung hard at the window, shattering the glass all over Vakeita. Reaching in, Zeek hit the unlock switch and opened the door.*

*"Get the fuck outta the car, bitch!" Zeek growled.*

*Vakeita gripped the steering wheel with both hands screaming, "I ain't giving up my car for fucking nobody!"*

*She did not have a mustard seed of fear and totally disregarded the weapon her child's father had been murdered with two months prior, during a drug deal gone bad. His mother had tried to take the car from her son after. Then she had a run-in with his brothers and sisters concerning the car. Now this! The car meant a lot to her and was her only transportation.*

*Zeek grabbed a handful of Vakeita's sandy reddish hair, snatching her out of the car. She came out swinging and hollering at the top of her lungs. She missed Zeek's face, but she hit him in the chest, clawing wildly with her fingernails. They dug in, leaving five long marks on Zeek's chest, which started bleeding immediately. As he threw her to the pavement, some of the blood splattered on Vakeita's white sundress.*

*"Fuck!" raged Zeek, as he gave her a swift kick in the chest, causing her 160-pound body to lay spread out on the parking lot.*

*Hammer did not like how the operation was going down. Yeah, he was down for the crown, but that did not include assaulting a pregnant sister. He stood there helpless, and as he looked at Vakeita lying on the ground, his tough-man image went straight out the window.*

*"Oh, my stomach hurts," Vakeita cried out.*

*Hammer knelt down beside her, "Please just stay down, and I promise I'll call an ambulance on the way out of here."*

*Zeek brushed the broken glass out of the car seat and fired the car up. "Nigga, let's get the fuck outta here," he commanded his partner.*

*Still, on the ground, Vakeita was sobbing, "Please, don't take my baby, please, don't take my child!"*

*Zeek already had the car in drive and was about to pull off when Hammer ran up to the car. The baby stared at him with a hateful glare from the rear car seat carrier.*

*"Man hold the fuck up. Let me get this baby out the fucking car! Old wild ass nigga!" Hammer said, as he unlatched the car seat. "A nigga ain't trying to catch a fucking kidnapping charge on a humbug."*

*When he handed the baby to Vakeita, she whispered a*

*polite, "Thank you."*

*"Ms Lady, you are most welcome," Hammer replied.*

*Zeek reached over the seat to slam the door closed. "Fucking soft ass nigga ...I'll meet you back at the spi-zi-zot," he said, with an attitude.*

*Spinning out of the parking lot, he headed down the highway. Zeek had not even gone a mile when he came up to a line of stopping traffic. Zeek immediately knew what was happening. Every month the law enforcers set up road-blocks to check for licenses, insurance, and registration, and he had just been unlucky enough to run up upon the damn thing. They had set it up, so that there were no streets or driveways to turn off onto without the cops seeing what exactly you were doing. Trying to avoid them, Zeek only had one choice, plan B. He pulled the burgundy Lexus over to the side of the road, popped the hood, and turned on the hazard lights. After looking under the hood for a minute, he closed it. Zeek took one more look at the car and calmly deserted it, walking up the road like he was headed to the nearest gas station.*

Vakeita was the first to speak when they came out of their past. "Zeek, I would like to thank you for saving my son. I remember when you took my car ...

Zeek Bey intruded on her statement, "Sister, I sincerely apologize for my wrongful doings." He paused and thought of the meaning of atonement.

What is the holy day of atonement?

Atonement is the seeking of forgiveness and guidance from Almighty God. The process of atonement includes recognizing the wrong and acknowledging the wrong, confessing to it, repenting from it, atoning for it, forgiving, reconciling and making a perfect union with Almighty God. Please note, however, that the process begins with recognition. We must recognize the value of human life.

Atonement is the prescription for moral and spiritual renewal. Black, Hispanic, Native-American, Asian, Pacific Islander, and White American families should engage in the eight steps of atonement.

Eight Steps of Atonement

1. Someone must point out the wrong.
2. Acknowledge the wrong.
3. Confess the fault. First to God, then to those offended.
4. Repentance - A feeling of remorse, contrition, and shame for the past conduct, which was wrong and sinful.
5. Atonement - meaning to make amends and reparations for the wrong.
6. Forgiveness by the official party - to cease another for the harm done.
7. Reconciliation and restoration - meaning to become friendly and peaceable again.
8. Perfect union with God.

"Vakeita, this was my destiny. God is the best of planner. If I could sacrifice my life all over again for your son, I would," Zeek Bey stated. "Faith without works is dead. I am one of God's vessels."

Before Vakeita could reply, the hood's Big Momma #1 and Big Momma #2, entered the hospital room carrying baskets of food. The hood's Big Daddy was carrying a red velvet cake and pecan pie. Several more people came in to show Zeek Bey love and support, as well as to pay their respect. They treated him as family.

"Momma, ya'll did not have to go through all this trouble by cooking all this food for me," Zeek Bey said, to Big Momma #1. Out of respect, he called all elder women *Momma*.

"Son, you did not have to risk your life for that kid either," Big Momma #1 said, as she patted his hand. "But you did though."

"Son," Big Momma #2 began fussing, "Shut your mouth boy. This home cooking will do you good. Now eat up, cause you not going to deny us our blessing. This here is God's work."

"Yes ma'am," Zeek Bey slobbed out, as his mouth got watery.

## CRIMINAL DAYS IS OVER

No more days of lookin' over my shoulder,
No more ungodly activities to go into the B.O.P. folder.
God is my provider, God is my only guide.
I'm a soldier for my merciful Lord; I'm his rider.
Every knee shall bow, every tongue shall confess.
I pray so much, now I'm not so heavy in the chest.
When I think of breaking any of God's rules, it scares me; unlawfulness was not my destiny.
To walk that walk and to talk that talk,
Oh Lord, help me, my flesh is weak, continue to strengthen me.
You lighten my burden, and restore my soul
Lord, you're head of my life, my mind and body is yours, please take control.
What is my purpose? I know I'll always be tested…
Put me under your powerful wings, and against all evil, protect me.
I mean your sacrifice. I'll worship you sincerely, whole-hearted, with all my life. Now I'm tired of rolling the dice with my life.

# CHAPTER 24

While Chase was getting processed out, Marvin Sapp song flowed out of the radio.

"He saw the best in me, when everyone else around me only saw the worse in me."

"Can I get a witness?" Officer Creed asked.

"I can say amen to that," Officer Bru, Bru said.

"Do you believe in God?" Officer Creed asked Chase.

"Whole heartedly," he responded.

Officer Creed pushed the paper in front of Chase to sign. "Young man, you know that we have to have a hair sample, so that we will always have your DNA on file."

"No problem," Chase said. He did not care what they needed from him or needed him to do, because once they finished, he could hit the gates. His mother and baby brother were in the parking lot at 7:30 a.m, when they clearly advised Chase to notify his family, they needed to be in the parking lot by 8:30 a.m. Better early than late, his mother thought.

"Bru, Bru. You made Godhead of your life." officer Bru, Bru asked Chase.

"Yes, sir."

"He saw the best in me, when everyone else around me only saw the worse in me," Officer Creed hummed, then put the words into the air. "Young man, what do you think about that song? You think that's a beautiful song?"

"Very powerful," Chase stated, "and so true."

"That's right," encouraged Officer Bru, Bru. "Speak on it. Tell the truth and shame the devil."

"Young man," Officer Creed began questioning Chase, "what you see so beautiful and powerful about that song?"

"What I see that is so extraordinary and so amazing about that song?" Chase asked himself, as he looked at the officer's name tag and addressed him by Officer Creed, "I am going to leave you with something, and hopefully you will pass it on. God knew us before we became a physical being, we came as a spirit being to live in human experience. Everything that you and I have done and will do in the future, God has already ordained it."

"Speak Bru, Bru."

"Saul was a cold killer in the Bible. Yeah, once Paul made that transition, he began to preach the word like never before. People learn from things; they go through transitions. When one knows better, one will do better. It dosesn't make you a bad person by one not working without love. When we don't know any better, we'll become who people turn us into. As we get older, we will take out the elements of who we are not."

"Our God gives gifts, cause God gives everyone gifts. God never gives up on us. Sometimes, it takes someone else to bring the best out of us. Nobody is exempt from some tough experience. Some people turn their experience into learning experiences. They are the ones who redeem themselves. The ones who go through experience, if there is no love, then there is no hope."

"Their demeanor has no love, they give no love, don't want no love, and at the end of the day, they will not receive any love. Until we understand the difference between a male and a man, we will always be confused."

"A male will always shame at what he is supposed to condole. They will see weakness where strength is, and strength where weakness is. Always remember, they only hide behind masks, many different masks. Now to add on to your question, It's good in us all, who determines when it surfaces? God and only God? God fixes us when he is ready."

"Walk with God young Brother," Officer Creed said.

"Bru, Bru, God takes care of his own people," Officer Bru, Bru claimed.

"Like he does to the babies and the fools," Chase added.

"Believe, believe, believe," Officer Creed mumbled.

"If there was no God, then there would be no me," Chase said, while giving Officer Creed a serious look. "I know God has never abandoned me, never forsaken me."

"Preach on, young brother," Officer Creed encouraged.

"Bru, Bru, if there was no God, there would be no us," Officer Bru, Bru corrected. "Just like there is a will, there is always gonna be away."

"A lot of great disciples, preachers, and wise men came from prison. Sometimes, this is where God have to allow one to be placed to be able to give him the Revelation," Chase said and saluted the officers. He was ready to get on the other side of the gates. To see what other plans God had in store for him. And for some strange reasons, Marvin Sapp other songs would not stop wrestling with his conscience and soul. So he began to allow the words to roll off his tongue, "I never would've made it, without you, Lord. Now I'm stronger; I'm wiser, I'm better. Without you Lord, I would've given up, Lord, you helped me out of my mess."

The powerful message lubricated his two ears and his body, and his conscience began to rest. He felt more peaceful within himself, as he continued to inhale and exhale the beautiful smell of freedom.

There is Some Good in the Worst of Us...
And Some Bad in the Best of Us…
Therefore, it Behooves Anyone of Us to

Find Fault with the Rest of Us.

# CHAPTER 25

Seven days after Sten X went home, Conscious was going to the laundry to exchange his sheets. Shakur decided to tag along for the exercise. Conscious was telling him about when he asked Mr. Jay why he did not tell him that his celly, Damage, was slow. Mr. Jay told Conscious he would have discovered that, as soon as Damage begin to run off his mouth.

"Damage's slow, but he's a good person," Shakur said.

"Shakur, my celly said when you watch women on TV too long, you fornicate," Conscious said, laughing.

This was something that he could not keep to himself. He used to get mad at Damage, but now he uses his time offering his celly because he was good and stupid.

"He meant lust, didn't he?" Shakur asked, enjoying the laugh.

Conscious exchanged his two sheets. He looked over his sheets before exiting the laundry. One of the sheets had blood on it. He pushed it back to the guy, "This sheet has blood on it, let me get another one." The brother gave him a look, as if he had an attitude, as he passed over the sheet. Conscious overlooked the sheet. The painter used it to catch paint from getting on the floor. Conscious showed the laundry officer.

"Its clean," the laundry officer said aggressively.

The laundry begin issuing dark brown towels, T-shirts, socks, face rags, and sheets, to hide the half-clean cloths. All the laundry clothes has to be full of dirt unless you had a laundryman.

Shakur exchanged his old clothes for his 6-month new issues. He was talking to the laundry officer, one of the laundry workers got in Shakur's video. Shakur respected the laundry workers hustle and fee, but he's a convict and went to get his proper issues for free. “Excuse me. Excuse me!” Shakur had to say to the worker because he was walking into their conversation without saying excuse me. The brother actually thought he ran the laundry.

“Main man, I am addressing my issue with the CO. You can continue to run your house, but right now, I am talking to the real boss.”

When Shakur finally made it back to his unit, the officer told him to go and see the secretary. Once in her presence, she delivered the beautiful news. “Shakur Douglas, today you are a free man. Your case has been overturned. On the two o’clock move, report to R&D. If you don’t report to R&D, that means that you like it here and would be happy to stay here a little bit longer.”

“A’hamdu lillaah.”

“Par me?”

“I said all praise be to Allah,” Shakur said, with a straight face, “this is my reward from Allah.”

“Douglas, I was told to give you a phone call, so you can share the good news with your family.”

“Thank you, but that won't be necessary. I want to surprise them.”

“Douglas, ain’t God good?”

“Allah is the most merciful and the head of my life… my guider and my protector.”

On the 2 o'clock institution move, 1400 guys walked Shakur to R&D, because they were his family, his brothers from different mothers. Soon as he received the lovely news, Shakur stayed on the rec yard the entire time. The guys treasured and cherished every single minute that they had left on the clock. Majority of them did not even report back to their jobs. Conscious valued Shakur’s presence the most, Shakur would bail out all the people with his knowledge. He never disappointed them, always freed them of their burdens. He was no yes man, Shakur always gave you the truth, whether you liked it or used the advice. Shakur thanked Allah that he was able to offer his last congratulations salat with his Sunni Muslim brothers.

---

The preacher man must have woken up on the wrong side of the bed, because he was having an extremely bad day. When today was supposed to be a very important day. He was looking forward to the speaking engagement at the college campus. He woke up late with a headache, probably due to missing his morning cup of coffee.

His front tire caught a flat, now he sat patiently at the bus stop, while waiting for the bus to arrive. "Lord, this is my first speaking engagement and everything that could go wrong, went wrong. I don't know if it is you testing me, or the devil trying to steal my joy, Lord. I am your servant and am here to do your will, and your will alone. Lord, I obey your signs and your symbols. Lord, you lead, and I shall follow. Amen."

As soon as he brought his prayer to a close, the bus arrived. "Lord, looks like we are going to make it on schedule after all," the preacher said, as he was climbing the few feet of steps onto the bus. After making the deposit, he looked around for a seat, and there was only one available. He frowned upon seeing the Muslims sitting directly across from him. The preacher's day began to get worse. His headache increased. His pattern of thinking went straight to the left; all negative thoughts flooded his brain. *Oh, Lord, please don't allow this guy do anything crazy! Take the bus for hostage or blow us all up.* The preacher man thought, while he made the small crazy prayer to God.

The earth, wind, and fire song came to Shakur's mind,

as he constantly watched the preacher glance at him. "Ain't it funny how your feelings show up on your face, no matter how hard you try to hide it. State your case."

*It is obvious the good Rev's making accusations, without evidence of any bad character traits on my part, seeing that he has never seen me before, nor having no knowledge of me*, Shakur thought. *Let me cut through this chase.*

"Morning Rev, how are you today?" Shakur asked, and began, giving the Rev the benefit of doubt. "You seem a bit nervous about tending to your flock this morning?"

"Why you say that, young man?"

"Like any good shepherd, we have to worry about the flock, there always one that tends to stray."

"Amen to that," the Rev said, in a surprised voice. Now the Rev begins to reprocess his initial thoughts of negativity towards Shakur. In fact, he was beginning to feel a bit foolish for profiling this young man, for no reason. Giving into his fear of ghost, thinking terrorists are coming out of the closet and behind every rock.

"Young man, I have a very delicate question I would like to ask you?"

Shakur had been waiting on that very delicate question, because it would tell him why the good Rev was giving him the sneaky and deranged looks. "Get it out of your system by all means."

"Why does the Muslims do those insane activities, all around the world?"

"Good Rev, what about when the Christians were killing people back in the day? Did you give your religion a full thorough investigation? The Christians were not only killing the people, they were also stealing their land. Telling them that if they didn't reannounce their religion and convert into the folds of Christianity, they would all die. The Christians slaughtered many and wasted tons of innocent blood."

The good Rev could not believe his ears, because what Shakur was stating was so true. No one had ever touched Christian history as Shakur has just unfolded. "Young brother, how did you become so knowledgeable? When did you find time to study history so deep?"

"I am just being released from prison. I always pray and ask Allah to increase me with knowledge," Shakur said, as he looked out through the bus's window. The real world was so beautiful to him.

"Our heavenly father will not allow the chosen ones to be held in bondage," said the Rev. Shakur went on and shared something with the good Rev out of the Qur'an. He told him about the surah that advised the Muslims to take and make the Christians their friends. Shakur clearly stated, that all people of faith would be considered his family. He also shared about how Sten X and Zeek Bey were into different religions, yet put their religious differences to the side and came together for the cause, and that cause was to be a soldier; a servant to the Lord. He also told the Rev about Big Buck and Tie, how they were Christians, how he loved them, as though they came from the same womb.

"Young man, you are exuberant."

"Yes sir, I am full of high spirits," Shakur agreed, smiling.

"What is your name, young man?"

"Shakur."

"Well Shakur, I am on my way to the college to speak to the youth. It would be a blessing if you were able to take advantage of this opportunity as well because you are a remarkable man."

Shakur did not say yes or no. He just went to talking. "Our young people think that it is cool to be bestial."

"Please elaborate, young man," the 66-year-old Rev. said. He wasn't ashamed to allow a youngster to educate him. Shakur has something that every wise person was supposed to seek from the womb to the tomb. *Knowledge*. Besides, a wise man always seeks wise counsel. "Bestial means like a beastly savage."

"I understand," the Rev nodded, as he blocked out everyone and everything among him and focused only on Shakur.

"Our young people are not exercising their aptitude," Shakur said, with sadness in his eyes and voice.

"What does aptitude mean?"

"A natural talent, quickness in learning." Once Shakur said that, he went on, "Our youth are afraid to change. So was I, until Allah removed the disease from my heart. I became vicissitude, which means changeability, a sudden or unexpected change within a person's life."

"Son, that was God's work."

"Allah is the best planner, and everything in life was ordained by Allah and Allah alone."

"Shakur, you are a very knowledgeable man."

"Please, don't give me credit, because all the credit goes and belongs to Allah," Shakur stated.

The good Rev knew that Shakur loved Allah, but he did not know Shakur made a covenant with Allah, and he looks to Allah for everything. Allah and Allah alone was Shakur's provider and protector, and Shakur prayed about everything, good or bad as well as standing before Allah, calling out to Allah, crying to Allah. Shakur depended on Allah, as an infant depends on its mother.

"Shakur, I can use a few good men such as yourself," the good Rev. admitted. "You, your brother Sten, and Zeek are the triad brothers," the good Rev. smiled. "Which means a group of three."

"I like that," Shakur smiled.

"Shakur?"

"Yes, good Rev?"

"How do you spell that word *vicissitud*?"

"V-i-c--i-s-s-i-t-u-d-e," Shakur spoke the words in slow motion.

"Thank you, son," the good Rev said. "Shakur, you will make an extraordinary speaker. You are fully aware that knowledge is meant to be passed on and not taken to the grave with us."

The good Rev so true statement got Shakur back into his jewel dropping beast mode. He shared with the good Rev. about when Allah commanded the angels to go and destroy a city, and the angels reported back to Allah and asked, "Why do you want the city to be destroyed, and did he know that there was a temple full of knowledgeable monks?"

"Allah told the angels that he knew all things, and what good does it do to give the people the knowledge, if they don't share it. Therefore, they are already dead."

"Shakur, are you going to join me at the college?"

Shakur thought about when he went to Reggie for assistance with winning back his freedom. Shakur answered the good Rev's question with the words that rolled of Reggie's tongue, "I am a tool in God's hands. I am a vessel. This is God's work, and I am nothing but a servant." And then Shakur added his own words, "How could I not, when it will be pleasurable to Allah, as well as the will of Allah. Allah makes us a blessing so that we can become a blessing to others."

---

All my peeps doing a bid. Speak out, so the younger generation can feel your pain... our incarcerated numbers gotta change. Long sentences, long bids, is surely not what we want for our kids.

The system robbed me out of my youth. Now it's time to tell nothing, but the whole truth. Let's wake up the youth.

We 're dying out like dinosaurs and gettin' swallowed up by Jaws, and my peeps, y'all still trying to ball. It's a hell-of-a fall.

Crimes don't pay. They upgrade technology by the day. Whitney Houston said she believed the kids are the future.

Teach them well, and let them lead the way… now all we gotta do is be honest with them, and tell them crime don't pay.

The people are on a serious mission about putting us all back into the servitude condition.

The penitentiary is a billion-dollar business. Let's not let the penitentiary be our tradition.

# About The Author

Prison gave me something that I never would've found as a free man. It gave me the opportunity to unfold and utilize my God given talents. We street guys would say that the prison saves the drug addict, but it also saved me. What doesn't kill us, will only make us stronger, and that's what it did for me. During my years working on a modern slave plantation, I realized I was leaning on my own understanding. For many, many years, I was standing in my own way and blocking the blessings that God had for me.

Throughout my 24 years in prison, I learned patience and persistence. However, I still feel the global streets' fallen soldiers' pain. It is a part of me. Stop digging the hole deeper for yourself. Let's try to curve some sense of unity and direction, as well as learn to strengthen and encourage one another. Because behind the wall, we're all that we've got. Real soldiers understand that violence is not always the answer. Satan, the devil, is out to destroy us all. We have to learn to stop fearing a change and learn to embrace that change.

# COMMENTS

I would like to exercise this blissful opportunity to share with you readers what some of my other reader's perspectives were, concerning my work. I welcome any comments as well.

With a brilliant stroke of a pen, the author has provided us with a bird's eye view of what has transpired in many homes across the country. A Daughter's Cry produces real-life experiences that break your heart, burden your mind, yet, warms the soul. Austin P. has created a masterpiece so eloquently written, about America's child.

Alan B. Austin A-Tampa Legend

Art is a form of expression, and writing is a form of art. It's good to give readers what they want, but it's not good to take away from yourself, at the same time. This is one of the reasons I enjoy reading Big Brother Austin's books. He shows just how versatile of a writer he is. His talent is a gift from Allah. In his stories, he promotes the growth of people, which is a key to life. Man must not confine one's mind to one thing. Knowledge is in all things. I challenge all readers to read this book and its entirety, and see if you do not feel enlightened about yourself. I give accolades to Brother Austin for promoting awareness of self and positive points of change. May the most high of the universe be pleased at his work, in promoting his will of perfection.

Rico Bias – Baltimore's Finest

As leaders, one's greatest responsibility to the youth is the reproduction of self. That is to reproduce ourselves by instilling within the hearts and minds of our youth our most constructive and positive qualities, recognizing that with every upcoming generation, it's becoming more and more acceptable to dishonor, deceive, betray, and sell out one another. Men! We have to make that change that we have been hoping to see. Brother Austin is trying to convey that message through his titles. I challenge everyone to support Austin on his journey to educating the message through his craft, which I find intriguing as food for thought. May God continue using your imagination for this purpose, and raise you higher in every area of your life.

John Lockett

To my very positive brother, Austin P. They say writing is therapeutic and good for the soul. Transformation part one and two are good for the writer, as well as the readers. It challenges you and makes you question your role in society, "Am I making society better or worse?" The writer is giving back in a very unique way by writing positive, urban novels and trying to reach those who need it the most. If you don't stand for something, you will fall for anything. My brother, Austin P, is standing for what is positive, Right and true and after reading these novels, I am standing with him. God bless you brother and keep fighting the good fight. After reading your novels, you have helped transform my way of thinking and living. I thank you for that.

Rock Chi-Town Finest

Brother Austin P is excellent in reading. It speaks truth to wrong. It shines light on darkness. A Daughter's Cry is a must-read book. It's a book that will touch your soul. We need more writers, such as Austin P, one that knows our black struggles. One that lives the life of a true convict, One that desires to see his people become more instead of less in life. Reading this brother's writing opened my eyes to the truth. I encourage whoever is reading my words to purchase any of the books written by Brother Austin P. Trust me, you will enjoy your journey through and through.

In closing, I desire to warn all my young black brothers. Know that your black skin is other's sins. Know that the foes have set traps to entrap you to come to jail. Know this truth; you are wanted dead or alive. I say to you brothers, come off that path of darkness that only leads you to jail or Hell. Get your education. It's the key to your success in life's struggles. Be the knower that knows their every move. Be that thinker that never thinks too late. It's enough, blacks doing things inside the devil's den of sin. Don't join us. May God bless you all. Power to the people.

Toke 2016

# Available Now

# Coming Soon

FEED THE
BEAST
A. PLAY

FEED THE
BEAST
A. PLAY

OPPORTUNIST
A. PLAY

A. PLAY

TRENDSETTER
A. PLAY

TRENDSETTER
A. PLAY

TRENDSETTER
A. PLAY

# Order Form

Make **Money Orders** PayableTo:
KBA Publications
PO BOX 2863
Phenix City, AL 36868

| QTY | KBA Publications Available | Price |
|---|---|---|
| | A Daughter's Cry | $15 |
| | Career Criminal | $15 |
| | Ridaz – Part II of Career Criminal | $15 |
| | Trans-4-ma-tion Part I | $15 |
| | Trans-4-ma-tion Part II | $15 |
| | Atl's Finest Part 1 | $15 |
| | Atl's Finest Part II | $15 |
| | Port City Playaz | $15 |

**Ship To:**

Name:
______________________________________________

Address:
______________________________________________

City: _______________ State: _______________ Zip: _______________

For Shipping and Handling: Add $3.75 for 1st Book. Add $1.75 for each additional book. All books are also available on Amazon and Kindle. All titles coming soon, also can be pre-ordered.